ROGUES' HOLIDAY

ALSO BY MARGERY ALLINGHAM

Blackkerchief Dick
The White Cottage Mystery
The Crime at Black Dudley
Mystery Mile
Look to the Lady
Police at the Funeral
Sweet Danger
Death of a Ghost
Flowers for the Judge
The Case of the Late Pig
Dancers in Mourning
The Fashion in Shrouds
Black Plumes
Traitor's Purse
Dance of the Years
Coroner's Pidgin
More Work for the Undertaker
The Tiger in the Smoke
The Beckoning Lady
Hide My Eyes
The China Governess
The Mind Readers
Cargo of Eagles
The Darings of the Red Rose

NOVELLAS & SHORT STORIES

Mr. Campion: Criminologist
Mr. Campion and Others
Wanted: Someone Innocent
The Casebook of Mr Campion
Deadly Duo
No Love Lost
The Allingham Casebook
The Allingham Minibus
The Return of Mr. Campion
Room to Let: A Radio-Play
Campion at Christmas

NONFICTION

The Oaken Heart: The Story of an English Village at War

AS MAXWELL MARCH

Rogues' Holiday
The Man of Dangerous Secrets
The Devil and Her Son

ROGUES' HOLIDAY

MARGERY ALLINGHAM
writing as
MAXWELL MARCH

OPEN ROAD
INTEGRATED MEDIA
NEW YORK

Copyright © 1935 by Margery Allingham

ISBN: 978-1-5040-9235-7

This edition published in 2024 by Open Road Integrated Media, Inc.
180 Maiden Lane
New York, NY 10038
www.openroadmedia.com

ROGUES' HOLIDAY

MURDER?

"WE LEFT HIM just as he was found, Inspector." Lieutenant Colonel Bloom's military training could not control the agitation in his voice. He stood, plump and breathless, looking up at the young man in front of him.

It was eleven o'clock on a bright June morning; the sun streamed through the tall Queen Anne windows of the Senior Bluffs Club, St. James's, lending that austere stronghold of old-fashioned wealth and snobbery a certain warmth and dusty splendour.

But even this added grace did not dispel the atmosphere of chill alarm which had already spread throughout the building in spite of every effort at secrecy.

This was not extraordinary, however, for a young man whose name had been entered on the club books at his birth, and whose election had been sponsored by two of the most distinguished names in the country, had committed the appalling breach of good taste of dying in a club bedroom; and, moreover, of dying in a most plebeian fashion, with the crevices of the windows stuffed with paper and the tap of the old-fashioned gas fire turned full on.

At best it was suicide.

Colonel Bloom, the resident secretary, did not like to think of the alternative.

The fact that there might possibly be an alternative accounted for the presence of the young Scotland Yard man who now stood looking down at the mound on the bed over which a departing doctor had reverently spread a sheet.

Inspector David Blest was young for his job and looked even younger than he was. The superintendent used to refer to him as "the chiel amang us." Brains, determination, and a quality which can only be described as dogged obstinacy had got him where he was, and although his blue eyes were lazy there was something behind them which gave those of his acquaintances who had something to hide a most uncomfortable sensation.

For the rest, he was uncommonly tall, fair-haired, lean, and not unhandsome.

At the moment he looked a trifle sleepy, and Colonel Bloom, who did not know him, made the mistake of feeling relieved.

"You see how it happened, Inspector," he said in his high-pitched voice, which became squeaky in moments of stress. "Pure accident. It's most unfortunate, of course. A terrible scandal for the club. Terrible. There will have to be an inquest, I suppose?"

David Blest glanced at him in mild surprise, and the hope died in the Colonel's eyes.

"Well, naturally," said David Blest, and went on speaking, still in the same slow pleasant tone which was one of his most charming characteristics. "Just let me run over the points again. The dead man is Eric Ingleton-Gray, of no occupation, twenty-seven years of age and unmarried—"

"A man about town," murmured the Colonel. "Such a good family, Inspector. His uncle, you know—"

"Quite," said David gently. "We needn't worry about that now. He doesn't need much influence to get him into his present club, I'm afraid, Colonel."

The resident secretary made a noncommittal if somewhat explosive sound, and the younger man continued patiently:

"He came to bed at twelve-thirty last night. We have the evidence of the senior valet for that. And he was drunk, I understand; so drunk that the old man says he put him to bed."

"There you are," said the Colonel excitedly. "A plain case. Ingleton-Gray was a young rip—I admit that. He must have stumbled out of bed, turned on the gas jet by accident, and there you are. Poor feller."

A faint smile passed over David's face.

"Do you usually keep the windows of your bedrooms stuffed up with newspaper, Colonel?"

"No," said the other man doggedly. "But it might have been an accident."

"Think so?" said Inspector Blest, and went on with his résumé. "The door was found locked this morning. Do members usually lock their doors in the club?"

"Good heavens, no, sir! What do you think this is? A hotel?"

The Colonel seemed to be in danger of losing his temper. But he quieted down after a moment or so.

"Perhaps you're right about suicide," he said. "The key was picked up in the courtyard, under the window. He must have locked himself in, thrown it out, and stuffed up the windows afterwards; a sort of safeguard to prevent himself funking it at the last moment and rushing out to safety. Poor feller. He was in very low water financially—between ourselves."

David Blest nodded absently. His eyes had strayed to the key which had been brought up by a hotel servant and laid upon the mantelpiece. It had been the finding of this key which had led to the uncovering of the tragedy, but as David looked at the little instrument he could not help feeling it was a great pity that so many people had handled it since its first discovery in the yard.

The Colonel had opened his mouth to speak but had been interrupted by the arrival of a page boy with a note. With a murmured word of apology he read it and stuffed it into his pocket.

The page, a small boy of fourteen or so, did not go, however. He hung about, an uncomfortable expression on his little peaky face, his eyes fixed in terrified fascination on the sheet-covered mound on the bed.

Colonel Bloom turned on him sharply.

"What's the matter, boy? Run along. Tell Bassett I'll be down in a minute."

Still the boy did not move.

"I wondered if I ought to tell the inspector about Mr. Ingleton-Gray, last night, sir."

"Certainly not. Run along at once. The inspector's not interested."

Colonel Bloom appeared to be on the verge of apoplexy, but the damage had been done. David turned slowly and smiled at the boy.

"Oh, but I am," he said. "I'm interested in everything. What about Mr. Ingleton-Gray, son?"

The boy, realizing his mistake, glanced at the Colonel in terror, but that gentleman shrugged his shoulders resignedly.

"Get on with it," he said. "And don't tell any more than the truth."

Having received permission, the boy was only too anxious to talk.

"Last night, sir, about ten o'clock, I was in the corridor outside here when I saw Mr. Ingleton-Gray come out of a room with another gentleman. Mr. Ingleton-Gray was very red. I think he'd been drinking then, sir. The other gentleman said, 'Won't you reconsider your decision, Eric?' and Mr. Ingleton-Gray said, 'No. Good God, I've sunk pretty low but not as low as that.' Then he turned round and knocked the other gentleman down, sir."

"Did he, though?" said Blest, his eyes alight with sudden interest. "What happened then?"

"Mr. Ingleton-Gray went on downstairs. I think he went to the lounge to get something to drink."

The boy evidently realized that he had lost his job anyway and was determined to get his story out.

"Never mind about that," said David. "What did you do?"

"I helped the other gentleman up, sir. I thought it was funny that Mr. Ingleton-Gray should hit him, because he was an oldish gentleman, the other one, and Mr. Ingleton-Gray was quite young and much bigger."

"I see," said David. "And what was the other gentleman's name?"

"Really, Inspector, this isn't necessary."

Colonel Bloom could contain his exasperation no longer.

"This is monstrous," he continued. "The gentleman in question is an old and distinguished member of the club. I can't have him brought into this distressing affair."

"I'm afraid you must allow me my own opinion there, Colonel." David's tone was very gentle but very firm. "I must insist on the name."

The Colonel hunched his shoulders.

"If you must know, it was Sir Leo Thyn. I ought to have told you about this incident, Inspector, but I thought that if we could keep a suicide verdict out of the question it would be to the general good. As it is, you can see the state of mind young Ingleton-Gray was in.

"Go away!" he roared suddenly at the boy, who was still waiting. "Go away. You've done enough mischief already."

Blest smiled at the boy.

"Wait for me downstairs," he said. "I shall want your name and address," and added as the door closed behind the youngster, "I should like a word with Sir Leo, Colonel."

"If you really think it necessary, Inspector."

"I'm afraid I do, sir."

"But surely, Inspector, Sir Leo's reputation alone is sufficient to preclude the idea of his having anything to do with this affair."

"I should like to see Sir Leo."

"Oh, very well, Inspector. I'll see if he's in the club."

While the Colonel was gone David had time to consider Sir Leo Thyn. On the face of it the evidence he had just heard was extraordinary. Sir Leo was certainly not the sort of man one would expect to hear had been knocked down in a club corridor.

In the first place he was extremely well known. For many years senior partner in a great legal firm, he had now retired, spending half his time on his country estate and half in the club. He was reputed to be enormously wealthy. But although he gave vast sums to charity, and his letters to the press urging stricter surveillance of public morals were well known, there was something not altogether pleasant about the flavour of his name.

It occurred to David suddenly that he had never heard anything definite against him, but the fact remained that he was not altogether liked.

David was still racking his brains for any other odd scraps of information about the man when the Colonel returned, very pink and unfriendly.

"Sir Leo will see you, Inspector."

The young policeman was amused to see that he was taken by back ways, although of course he wore no sort of uniform. The Colonel was evidently anxious for the members of the Senior Bluffs to be protected from any reminder of the tragedy in their midst.

He led David to his own private sitting room, and, as the two men entered, a short, thickset figure rose from the leather armchair by the fire.

Although he had often seen photographs of the man, David had not before set eyes upon Sir Leo himself; therefore his appearance came as something of a shock to him.

Sir Leo Thyn's peculiarity lay in his colouring. He was a man of perhaps sixty-five or so, with a bright red face and closely cropped very white hair, which seemed to have something of a pinkish tinge since the skin beneath it was so rubicund. By contrast, his eyes were quite black and surprisingly sharp.

He pressed a large fat hand in the inspector's own, and when he spoke his voice was as easy and conciliatory as the Colonel's had been nervous and irritable.

"Good-morning, Inspector," he said. "Bloom here has been telling me that you want to know about my little contretemps with poor young Ingleton-Gray last night. Well, there's not much to be told, and I'm sorry it had to come out. Now the poor young fellow's killed himself it won't do his memory any good for it to be known that he knocked down a man old enough to be his father on the night he made up his mind to go to meet his Maker."

This opening, so frank and friendly, might have disarmed even a shrewder man than David had it not been for something in the very atmosphere of the man which the young inspector could not place. It was something quite intangible, something that might easily have been his own imagination, but he was conscious of it and it remained with him until the end of the interview.

He asked the formal questions. Sir Leo seemed only too anxious to oblige him. Yes, he knew Ingleton-Gray well. Yes, he himself had spent the night at the club in his own room some doors from the dead man's own.

It was only when they came to the actual subject of the conversation which Sir Leo had had with the dead man before the knocking-down incident that he showed any signs of reluctance.

"I don't see that this is necessary, Inspector, but as you insist," he said at last. "Young Ingleton-Gray was in serious debt. I happened to know that he owed his bookmaker a considerable sum, and there was another, more personal matter—a woman, as a matter of fact—who was claiming pretty heavy sums from him."

He paused, and David nodded.

"I am afraid I must ask why exactly you took Mr. Ingleton-Gray on one side last night," he said bluntly.

Sir Leo shrugged. "Well, it's very awkward," he said, "but if you must know, I offered to lend him some money." He hesitated. "Well, I wasn't even going to lend it to him. I was going to give it to him. To be quite honest, Inspector, it made me sick to see the way the boy was going, and I got hold of him and talked to him like a Dutch uncle and finally finished by offering to get him out of his difficulties on condition that he took a job and became a responsible member of society."

David's eyes narrowed.

"It strikes me as being rather extraordinary that he should have said, 'I've sunk pretty low, but not as low as that,' and then should have knocked you down, after such a kindly proposition on your part," he said slowly.

"So it did me," said Sir Leo. "So it did me, young man. But then you must remember the young fellow was half-crazed with drink, and perhaps I laid the lecture on too thick. You know, we old buffers, when we get going, we sometimes forget ourselves."

He smiled depreciatingly, and David suddenly decided that he disliked the man. However, he knew quite well that Sir Leo had only to go into a witness box and tell the same story to be believed completely.

He expressed his thanks, therefore, and took his leave, after completing the formalities with the club servants.

Some hours later he was standing in the superintendent's office at the Yard.

Old McQuirk, fatherly but superior in his dusty brown tweed suit, his appalling pipe stuck in the corner of his mouth, was laying down the law, as usual.

"I like you, David," he said, "but you're crazy. Remember you're a policeman, not a clairvoyant. Stick to facts: that's all the law asks of you. Window stuffed up, door locked, key in the yard outside the window, impecunious young man dead inside with the gas full on—that's suicide.

"Take my advice," he went on, wagging the stem of his pipe at the young man. "Don't make trouble when there isn't any. And make sure there is some when there is," he went on inconsequentially.

"All right, sir," said David, who knew the chief well enough to be neither offended nor even hurt by the homily.

He guessed also that the powers that be might have a personal interest in the fair reputation of the Senior Bluffs, while Sir Leo Thyn, he realized, was much too important a person to be considered suspect save on the strongest possible evidence.

However, he felt he had done his duty. He had pointed out most carefully that a man who was so drunk that he had to be put to bed might not be able to get up again to stuff a window and turn on the gas, even had such an unpleasant impulse occurred to him.

The chief went on speaking.

"I don't know what's worrying you," he said testily. "You've got a mania for work. You've got some leave coming, haven't you?"

"Yes, sir. A fortnight. It starts tomorrow."

"Well, then, run along, for heaven's sake," said the Old Man. "Run along and enjoy yourself. Be a little human for a change. Good-bye, my boy, and good luck to you. Ingleton-Gray was a suicide. You'll attend the inquest this afternoon and you'll see. Suicide, temporary insanity. The poor old Bluffs won't hold up its head again for years."

As Inspector Blest went out he reflected that everything the chief had said was in the nature of prophetic truth. He smiled to himself. Since the chief had not raised the subject and had evidently not wanted it to be raised, he had been tactful enough not to point out that because a key is found underneath a bedroom window it does not necessarily follow that it has been thrown from that window, but may quite easily have been placed there by someone who has locked the bedroom door from the outside.

As he went down the corridor to his own room a messenger brought him a note. It was from Jimmy Thorne, the page boy at the Bluffs, who had proved so informative earlier in the day.

David smiled as he read the note, and mentally put down another good mark against young Jimmy's record.

The note was by way of fulfillment of a charge he had given the boy in private before he left the club.

DEAR MR. INSPECTOR [it ran]: *The gent. you are interested in told Johnson to ring up and reserve him a suite at the Arcadian Hotel, Westbourne-on-Sea. Hope this finds you as it leaves me at present. Yours respectfully,* JAMES THORNE.

P.S. Thank you ever so much for fixing that I did not get the sack.

David put the note in his pocket. As he turned into his room a colleague greeted him.

"Hallo, David. Off on leave? Where are you going?"

Inspector David Blest grinned.

"Arcadian Hotel, Westbourne-on-Sea," he said.

2

COURTSHIP EXTRAORDINARY

W HY DON'T YOU go and 'ave a bathe, sir? Sea's lovely."
The old waiter in the lounge of the Arcadian Hotel
stood regarding the young man with patent concern.

For three days David had sat alone in the corner of the lounge
overlooking the glittering esplanade, and he was getting on Old
Charlie's nerves.

He glanced up and smiled at the man's suggestion.

"Think I'm bored?" he inquired.

Old Charlie had served the Arcadian in the days before the
splendour of its mighty new building had made it the Mecca of
those wealthy holiday makers who patronized the fashionable
south coast watering place of Westbourne-on-Sea, and he was a
privileged person.

All the same, he made haste to cover any infringement of
etiquette.

"Oh no, sir," he said. "Not at all, sir. Of course not, sir."

"Then you're wrong," David said, leaning back in the deep cane
chair. "I am bored. Bored stiff. I'm wondering why on earth I
came. The gilded life of the English pleasure seeker does not
appeal to me."

"Oh, don't say that, sir!" Old Charlie was shocked. "It's because you don't go in for it, if I may say so, sir. When I saw you the first day, sitting 'ere, I thought you was waiting for someone who 'adn't turned up."

David grimaced. The old man was not far out. Three days, three precious days, and there was no sign of Sir Leo, although a suite awaited him.

Old Charlie shook his head.

"If it was raining I could understand it," he said. "But it's lovely weather. Look at the sun on them red and white bathing tents. They're quite a picture. The Lido hasn't got anything on Westbourne this year. Why, we're filling up even this great place, sir. More coming every day. You ought to be about, enjoying yourself."

David shook his head, and the old man eyed him thoughtfully.

"Now—no offence, sir," he said at last. "No offence meant and none took, I'm sure. But if you—er—if you 'ad a *lady*, now, to go about with..."

David laughed outright.

"I don't like ladies," he said. "Don't worry about me."

"Don't like ladies, sir?" Old Charlie evidently gave the young man up as hopeless. "Well now, fancy that!"

Then an idea occurred to him as a possible explanation for this odd peculiarity in a young man.

"Perhaps there's one lady who's not 'ere, sir?" he ventured diffidently.

"No," said David, shattering his hope. "No lady anywhere, thank God."

"Well!" said Old Charlie in despair. "Well! I'll bring you a nice iced lager, sir." He padded off sadly.

David rose to his feet and wandered over to the reception desk, where he inquired somewhat forlornly if there were any messages for him.

He had received the usual answer and was idly turning over

some of the advertising matter spread out upon the desk when there was a little commotion behind him, and he turned to see a new arrival.

The porter came first, carrying two large suitcases, and behind him, leaning heavily on the arm of the commissionaire, was a girl who wore a squirrel coat wrapped tightly round her slender form, although the day was bright and hot.

The little procession came slowly up to the desk where he stood. As they came abreast of him the girl turned to her escort and dropped something into his hand.

"Thank you. I'm quite all right now," she said. "It was only getting in and out of the car fatigued me."

David was agreeably surprised. In his own private opinion most women had ugly voices: either two low and intentionally vibrant, or too high and liable to become shrill on the least provocation.

But this was something quite different. This was a nice voice; gentle but not consciously so, musical and unaffected.

He turned to look at the girl and was startled by the pallor of her face. Apart from this extraordinary paleness she was really very lovely, and the young man who had just said he did not like women found himself looking at her with more than common interest.

She was very fair, and small honey-coloured curls showed under the brim of her little hat. Her eyes were grey, with fine arched eyebrows, and her features really extraordinarily well chiselled.

David took in all these facts subconsciously. They were not things in which he interested himself, as a rule.

Consciously, he was fascinated by her fragility. She looked so weak, so extraordinarily pathetic, that instinctively he glanced round for the trained nurse who, he felt sure, must be in attendance.

She was quite alone, however, and presently he heard her speaking to the clerk.

"I am Miss Judy Wellington. I wrote to you about a room."

"Oh yes, Miss Wellington. Number forty-nine, on the first floor, overlooking the sea."

The clerk also seemed startled by her appearance.

David remembered the room number because it was next door to his own room, number fifty.

Old Charlie was waiting over by his chair with the iced lager, but he did not move.

The girl signed the register and was turning away when the clerk spoke awkwardly.

"Excuse me, but—er—I mean—are you all right, Miss Wellington? Could I ring for a maid to take you upstairs?"

A faint smile passed over the girl's face.

"Oh no, thank you," she said gently. "I'm quite all right. I'm a permanent invalid, of course, but I'm quite able to walk if I go slowly."

She turned away and followed the man with her bags, moving very slowly. The clerk looked after her.

"What a damned shame," he said impulsively, and David looked up. The remark had expressed his own thoughts completely.

He went back to his seat and sat sipping his drink thoughtfully, idly speculating about the girl.

After a moment or so he pulled himself together and reverted to the subject which until this moment had had all his attention: a possible alternative to the story Sir Leo Thyn had told him in the secretary's room at the Senior Bluffs, and what it could possibly have been that young Ingleton-Gray had not sunk low enough to do.

But the recollection of the girl returned to him. Presently he rose and walked out into the terrace garden and down the wide steps to the sea.

It was all very bright, very gay. Brown-skinned young women in the scantiest of costumes lay on brightly striped rugs in the sun; all rather like a revue, David thought.

He was going back through the hotel garden when for the first time since his arrival at Westbourne he caught sight of a figure he recognized.

The man was seated alone on one of the marble benches, surveying the horizon with much the same sort of lordly detachment which David himself had affected some minutes before. He did not see the inspector at once, and that young man had leisure to observe him.

He was a small man, fastidiously dressed, almost too fastidiously. There was a faint nattiness about him, a flavour of the over-smart, and David smiled to himself.

Johnny Deane, alias "the Major," was one of Scotland Yard's most frequent visitors. By profession he was a "con man," or confidence trickster, and a place like the Arcadian was just the sort of ground in which he preferred to work.

At the risk of spoiling Mr. Deane's holiday David wandered over and sat down beside him.

" 'Afternoon, Major," he said.

Mr. Deane turned round. For a moment his expression was a complete blank. Then he held out his hand.

"Well, if it isn't my old friend from the college," he said, betraying the soft voice and educated accent which was part of his stock in trade. "Well, well, well, how pleasant it is to run into people one knows.

"You're on holiday, I suppose?" he went on affably.

"You," said David placidly, "I suppose are on business?"

The Major smiled. "For once you're wrong," he said. "I hate to disappoint you, but for practically the first time in my life I have no need to work."

"Oh? Found a wealthy sucker?"

Johnny Deane blew a cloud of smoke into the air.

"No," he said. "No, quite seriously. I wish I could tell you all about it, but I can't. Not because you're a policeman, but because I can't tell anybody. I've got a job. Something easy, pleasant, with no risk attached. In fact, it's all completely aboveboard. Just a little favour for a gentleman I know, and between you and me, old man, it's going to see me sitting pretty for some time to come. Oh, I'm in clover."

David looked at the man and he had the odd impression that he was telling the truth. The Major seemed to divine his thoughts.

"It's a fact," he said. "I don't mind you hanging about, even. The man I'm doing this thing for knows my record, knows all about me. I haven't hidden anything from him. I tell you, I've had a bit of luck. I may even be able to go straight after this. When I get my flat in Brook Street you must come and have a drink with me some time."

David was interested. He did not believe such stories as a rule, but he knew that Johnny would not be sitting there so placidly by his side if he had anything of which to be afraid.

"It dropped right out of the air, this thing," Johnny said confidentially. "I only heard of it the day before yesterday. I was so hard up I thought I should have to go back to the old school for a bit, and then up comes this little job clean out of the air, and here I am, all set for a lovely holiday."

"Well, I hope for your sake it's on the level," said David, getting up. "Are you staying here, by the way?"

"No. I'm over at the Queen's. But I may move over to your place tomorrow or the day after. I hear the food's better. So long."

As David went upstairs to his room he was still thinking about the Major. He was a funny little chap, he reflected, and apart from his criminal habits really not a very bad sort of person. On the whole he was inclined to believe his story, and he wondered who on earth could find Johnny a job that was on the level and was yet suited to his peculiar taste.

At any rate, here was one little mystery. Even if Sir Leo did not turn up and he had to search for him elsewhere, his visit to West-bourne might not be entirely without interest.

Then he remembered the girl. It struck him as being peculiar even then that he could not get her face out of his mind.

He changed in a leisurely fashion, wondering in a vague sort of way if she would appear at dinner. A permanent invalid: it certainly was a shame; a damned shame with anyone as lovely as that.

He was in shirt and trousers when the crash came, one of the most tremendous thumps he had ever heard.

He paused, collar in hand, and listened.

There was silence for a moment, and then quite distinctly a small feminine moan.

It sounded so near that he started and looked about him in astonishment. The explanation was instantly apparent.

His own room and the room next door had been intended as part of a suite, so that there was a communicating door between them. The demand for single rooms being great, however, a small wardrobe had been placed over the door so that only the top part of the moulding was visible.

He hesitated. He was only partially dressed.

Suddenly it dawned upon him that the room where the crash had occurred must be number forty-nine. It must belong to the invalid girl.

It sounded as though a chest of drawers had turned over.

He felt that something ought to be done. His glance wandered towards the wardrobe.

In a moment he had wrenched it aside. It was empty and quite light.

It never occurred to him that the door beyond might have been left unlocked, but the moment his hand touched the latch it sprang open, and he found himself on the threshold of the room beyond.

The first thing he saw was that he had made a mistake. A

slender but athletic young person in a bathing suit was lifting an overturned chest of drawers back into position.

He saw instantly what had happened. She had been indulging in setting-up exercises, wedging her feet under the chest to pull herself into a sitting position. The chest, being empty, was light and had overturned.

All this took a moment, and he was just about to go back to his room when she turned her head.

Very few things surprised Inspector David Blest, but on this occasion his eyebrows rose and his mouth fell open, for the face which stared up at him, consternation slowly giving place to alarm on the lovely features, belonged to Miss Wellington, the permanent invalid of the reception hall, and, moreover, her pallor had completely disappeared.

This was a Miss Wellington who had never been an invalid in her life.

For perhaps two seconds their eyes met, and then David stepped back into his own room with a muttered word of apology and sat down on the bed. As he digested his astonishment he heard her lock the door, and the enormity of his behaviour suddenly dawned upon him.

And the girl had seen him and had certainly recognized him.

He sat there cursing himself for some time, and then it suddenly occurred to him to wonder what on earth she was doing.

Inspector Blest knew very little about young women not of the criminal class, but he knew enough to realize that permanent invalids do not indulge in strenuous physical exercises which upset chests of drawers.

In the end, however, he returned to his own side of the incident and determined to apologize at the first possible opportunity. He even waited up in his own room for an hour after he was fully dressed in the hope that he might catch her as she came out of her room.

In this, however, he was defeated, for she did not appear that evening, and it was not until he came up to his room the following morning, after searching for her in vain in the breakfast room, that he met her coming out of her bedroom and tottering slowly down the corridor towards the lift.

She was pale again. The extraordinary whiteness which he had noticed at their first meeting had returned. Moreover, although it was a broiling morning, she still wore the squirrel coat clutched tightly about her.

He saw that she recognized him, and she would have passed had he not stopped her.

"I say," he began awkwardly, "I feel I must apologize for my extraordinary behaviour yesterday. Only you see, I heard the crash, and I wasn't dressed, and I wondered if you—well, if someone was hurt." He hesitated and finished lamely: "I'm so sorry."

To his relief she did not snub him. Instead he found two grey eyes resting quizzically upon his face.

"You saw what I was doing?" she said.

"I ... saw you put the chest of drawers back, yes," he said.

There was a long pause, and then the inspector felt a light touch on his arm, a touch which startled him considerably.

"Don't," said a soft voice, "please don't tell anybody that I'm not ill, will you? Please—"

He was surprised at her tone, which was so near entreaty.

"No," he said impulsively. "No. All right, I won't."

The girl sighed. "Thank you," she said. "Thank you so much." She tottered off down the corridor, leaving him completely bewildered.

It was after lunch when he spoke to her again. All the morning she had sat in his favourite corner, and after lunch took up her position there again. She looked pathetic, and quite absurd in the circumstances, sitting there with her pale face and fur coat.

Finally he went over to her.

"Do you mind?" he said.

She hesitated. "Well, it is very dull here, isn't it?"

He sat down. They were alone, and no one was within earshot. He leaned forward.

"Aren't you extremely hot in that coat?"

She nodded. "Yes. Awfully."

David edged round to his subject.

"Look here," he said, "I don't want to be inquisitive, and honestly I'd rather do anything than be a nuisance to you, but is it absolutely necessary for you—to—well, to masquerade like this?"

She met his eyes squarely.

"Yes," she said. "Yes, I'm afraid it is. Please don't talk about it."

David hesitated.

"I only asked," he said at last, "because—well, I wondered if your—er—illness would still be necessary if you weren't in West-bourne. You see," he hurried on without giving her time to reply, "I've got a car. It's not a very good one, but I thought we might go along to Sandy Bay, which is about fifteen miles down the coast, and have a swim and come back."

The girl glanced out over the glistening water. The invitation was obviously attractive. On such a day few people could resist the appeal of that dancing water.

She looked at him. "I don't know you at all," she said.

"My name's David Blest," he said. "I don't know anybody here. I'm completely without friends or relations, and I would very much like to drive you down to Sandy Bay."

The girl glanced out across the sea once more. Then she rose to her feet.

"It's perfectly mad," she said. "But if you knew what this coat was like—Where's the car?"

At half-past five that evening, after the swim of a lifetime, David stopped the car at his passenger's request ten miles out of Westbourne.

"I'm sorry," she said, "but I can't attend to my make-up while we're jolting about. This has to be done very carefully."

David pulled up, and, leaning back in his seat, surveyed the girl at his side. For three hours crime and criminals had never once entered his thoughts.

They had not talked about the girl's affairs, by mutual consent, and for the first time in his life David had been content to let a mystery go unsolved.

Judy Wellington was not like any other girl he had ever known. She had intelligence and she had charm, and beauty, too, he thought, as he saw her sparkling eyes and flushed cheeks.

She opened the bag on her knees.

"Is this necessary?" he said.

For a moment all the amusement died out of her face, and there crept into her eyes something which he had seen there before and which he recognized only now. It was not surprise or fear, but, surprisingly, grim determination, determination to see something through, at whatever cost.

"Yes," she said, "I'm afraid it is," adding lightly, "My 'illness' is going to be a bit patchy. I'm afraid this stuff won't take very well after sea water."

"What is it?" he inquired.

She grimaced. "Frankly, it's called a beauty mask. It's stuff you're supposed to spread over your face at night and wash off in the morning. I discovered it ages ago. It makes me look very ill, don't you think?"

"Horribly," he said, and added abruptly, "I say, I wish you wouldn't do it."

She was grave again immediately.

"I wish I needn't, too," she said. "But I'm afraid I must. And look here, while I'm about it I'd like to thank you very much for this. You see, I don't suppose I shall see you again after today."

"But why not?"

She shook her head.

"I can't explain. You promised you wouldn't ask. You must wonder what on earth I'm doing, I know that, but I can't very well tell you all about it. One thing perhaps, though, I ought to explain. I've come to the Arcadian to meet the man I'm going to marry."

He stared at her, a completely unaccountable chill passing over him.

"Don't you know him?" he said at last.

"No," she said. "Not yet. My guardian's bringing him down some time this evening or tomorrow."

Inspector Blest felt suddenly and completely flat, so flat that he recognized that he was in danger of making a fool of himself and took refuge in lightness.

"Is this extraordinary performance for his benefit?" he inquired, indicating the cosmetic jar. "What's the idea? Are you arousing his protective instincts?"

"Don't," she said. "Please don't."

"Look here," he said, "can't I possibly help you in some way or other? I don't understand this business, and I don't want to inquire if you're anxious I shouldn't, but if there's anything I can possibly do—"

She shook her head, and he saw to his surprise and alarm that she was very near tears.

"There's nothing," she said. "Nothing at all. Now, really, please, I must get on with my makeup."

He watched her paint out most of her beauty and helped her into her heavy coat. Then she huddled up in the seat beside him.

"Now," she said, "please, as fast as you can. It's been a wonderful, wonderful day."

They entered the Arcadian together, the girl leaning lightly on his arm. Inspector Blest was amazed at himself. Her touch thrilled him, and her extraordinary story, far from filling him with mere curiosity, had poured over him an avalanche of gloom.

The lounge was crowded. New arrivals showed on every hand. They were halfway across the foyer when he heard a quick intake of breath at his side, and the arm which rested on his own trembled.

"Oh," said a small husky voice at his side, "there's my guardian! And that man with him, that, I suppose, is the man I've got to marry."

David turned his head and followed the direction of her eyes. The next instant he had stiffened, and a wave of utter incredulity and amazement passed over him, for edging his way through the tables toward them was the square figure of his own original quarry, Sir Leo Thyn; and behind him, a self-satisfied smirk on his not unintelligent face, was the last man in the world he expected to see—Johnny Deane, alias the Major.

Sir Leo came up to the girl.

"Judy, my dear," he said, "where have you been? Mr. Deane and I have been at our wits' end about you. And," he added, turning a stony glance in David's direction, "and who on earth, my dear, is this?"

For a moment after Sir Leo had spoken there was an uncomfortable pause. The hostility in the old voice was unmistakable, and the girl was quick to assimilate it. Before David could open his mouth she had answered.

"It was such a beautiful evening, Sir Leo, that I thought I would try to go for a stroll. But the exertion was too much for me. I felt very faint, and this gentleman most kindly brought me home."

For the first time since he had known her David was conscious of a thrill of alarm in her tone, and he realized intuitively that her need must be very great or she would never lie so glibly.

Sir Leo looked at her sharply, and David found himself hoping, most unprofessionally, that those quick dark eyes would not penetrate her extraordinary disguise.

"I see. Very kind of Inspector Blest, I'm sure." Sir Leo's sarcasm was biting. "However, now you're in safe hands, my dear, and next time you persuade a policeman to bring you home, choose one in uniform, not a plainclothes officer."

He drew the girl's arm through his, and for an instant his glance met David's own. The young man's lean brown face had turned a dusky crimson, and there was certainly now no trace of laziness in the very blue eyes. He controlled himself, however, and nodded stiffly. There seemed nothing he could say.

"A police inspector?" He hardly heard the words, they were uttered so softly.

He turned his head to find the girl looking up at him, and before the expression of dismay and reproach in her white face he was stricken helpless.

Sir Leo led his charge away, and David Blest stood looking after him. For the first time his official attitude towards life was completely undermined. At that moment, as far as Inspector Blest was concerned, the world held no other woman save Judy, and the one desire he possessed was to talk to her and explain.

The incident which pulled him together and restored his perspective was typical. Forgotten completely by the three participants in the little drama, Major Johnny Deane stood apart, and as the old man and his ward moved off down the foyer he hesitated whether to follow them or to make an overture to the inspector.

David found the man's eyes resting on his face with that half-diffident, half-speculative expression which he had seen before in the faces of so many crooks.

Acting on the inspiration of the moment, the young policeman smiled.

"Watch out, Johnny, my lad," he said softly. "Watch out."

Then, with newly found purpose, he strolled off out of the hotel to find a conveniently quiet telephone box from which to hold a long conversation with Scotland Yard.

THREE HUNDRED THOUSAND
POUNDS

Y OU ARE very silent, Major."

Sir Leo's booming voice was softened, but his eyes were not nearly so amenable. So far the meeting had hardly been a social success.

The three people sat in the drawing room of the luxurious and somewhat over-ornate suite, the best the Arcadian could provide. Two tall windows gave onto a balcony which overlooked the front, now glittering in the dusk with a thousand coloured lights, while the grey sea, warm and mysterious, reflected them again and again.

Still clutching her coat about her, Judy sat huddled up in an immense gilt and tapestry chair, her eyes fixed on the romantic scene outside the window in an absorbed, unseeing stare.

Sir Leo was plainly irritable. For half an hour now he had tried to give this meeting some semblance of the romance it should have possessed, but the two chief protagonists in the tragi-comedy had failed him. The girl was shrinking, weary, and silent, and the Major ill at ease, awkward, and a great disappointment to Sir Leo, who had expected much of him.

Lashed by the underlying irritation in the soft voice, the unfortunate Johnny Deane pulled himself together.

"Er—yes," he said, "I was telling Miss Wellington she can have no idea how pleasant a yachting trip in the Mediterranean can be at this time of year. I remember some years ago—"

He broke off. The girl had risen. She looked terribly pale and haggard, her small face peering out from the great collar of grey fur.

"Sir Leo—Major," she said, "I wonder if you would excuse me? I'm afraid I have overtired myself today. I usually go to bed very early. I don't wish to seem impolite, but—"

"Of course." The Major's alacrity was a little too spontaneous for true gallantry.

Sir Leo rose. "I will see you to your room."

She shook her head. "No, thank you. I'm quite all right. I'm so sorry to be so silly. Perhaps we could continue our talk in the morning?"

She steadied herself with an effort and controlled her shaking voice.

"By that time I shall be quite ready to do anything you suggest, Sir Leo."

She went out, very small, very dignified, and somehow extraordinarily pathetic. The high panelled door closed behind her, and they heard her high-heeled shoes clicking on the polished parquet of the corridor.

When the sound of her footsteps had died away Sir Leo spun round and faced the Major.

"Not good enough, Deane," he said sharply. "You'll have to play your part better than this. What's the matter with you?"

The bully in the man's nature had never showed more clearly than it did at that moment, and before the onslaught the unfortunate crook drew back. But, like many weak characters, there was a querulous, sly side to his temper, which suddenly blazed up.

"That's just what I was going to say to you," said Mr. Deane.

"What are *you* playing at? What's the big idea? When I came into this business I didn't know there was going to be a perishing inspector from Scotland Yard in on the ground floor. What are you doing? Trying to frame me?"

Sir Leo laughed, but the sound was not very convincing.

"Good heavens, is that what's worrying you?" he said.

He helped himself to a cigar from a box on the table and lit it before continuing.

"That policeman was an accident," said Sir Leo airily. "He must have met the girl, seen that she was feeling ill, and brought her along. It's just a coincidence, that's all."

"Do you believe that?" Johnny Deane was regarding his employer thoughtfully.

"Well, of course," said Sir Leo testily. "What else could it have been?"

"Policemen and coincidences don't go together," said the Major doggedly. "Not in my experience, anyway, and I've had plenty of both. And if it wasn't a coincidence, what was it? That's what I want to know. Are you trying to frame me?"

Sir Leo sank down in his chair and laughed.

"My dear good fellow, why should I go out of my way to do anything quite so futile and ridiculous? There's no need to have a fit of hysterics every time you see a policeman."

Johnny flushed. The thrust had gone home, but he was still far from being convinced.

"I don't like it," he said. "I'm superstitious, for one thing, and it's unlucky to see a policeman walking with the bird you're out to pluck."

Sir Leo frowned and broke the ash off his cigar into the tray on his table.

"I don't like your conversation, Deane," he said. "I don't like your mind. Good heavens, what have you possibly got to fear?"

"That's what I want to know," said Johnny Deane, coming forward. "And that's what I've got to know before I go on any further in the business. What am I letting myself in for? You've promised me twenty pounds a week for life as long as I remain married to that poor invalid kid you're responsible for. As long as I don't divorce her you guarantee that I needn't live with her or support her. That's the bargain, isn't it?"

"Yes," said Sir Leo without looking up. "That's it, my friend, and an extremely advantageous one from your point of view, if I may say so."

Johnny Deane was a crook of some experience, and whatever his other shortcomings might have been, he was not a complete fool. A faint smile spread over his ignoble countenance.

"Yes," he said softly. "A very good bargain for me. Almost too good. And when I say that, Sir Leo, I mean suspiciously good. When you put this yarn up to me you told me that you were very fond of the little girl, that you wanted to see her married. It made it sound as though you were something philanthropic. I didn't know you then as well as I do now, and perhaps I thought you were one of these rich eccentric old birds, not quite as steady on the top story as you ought to be.

"Look at it from my point of view, Sir Leo," he went on, changing his tone. "When you come down here I find you're not so keen on the girl as I'd supposed. No one seeing you with her for half a minute, you know, could imagine that you thought any more of her than you would of a stock or a bond in which you were interested. After we struck our bargain I come down here and hang about for you to arrive and introduce me to the lady, and when you do come, what do I find? 'There's the girl,' you say, and there she darned well is, on the arm of a blinking copper. No, I'm sorry, old boy, you've picked the wrong man."

Sir Leo, who had listened to this harangue in silence, an amused smile upon his lips, glanced up sharply on the last words.

"And what exactly do you mean by that, Mr. Deane?"

The question, put so quietly yet with such a force of interrogation behind it, pulled the Major up sharply. He fell back on bravado.

"Just exactly what I say, old man," he said, albeit somewhat uncomfortably. "Just exactly what I say. I'm through. I don't like the sound of the business as much as I did, and the bargain's off. You must get someone else to marry that kid of yours, for it's not going to be Johnny Deane. I've done all sorts of risky things in my life, but always with my eyes open. I'm not one of these guys who work in the dark. That's all I've got to say."

He paused uncomfortably. Sir Leo was not looking at him. He was leaning back in his chair, his eyes closed, puffing leisurely at his cigar.

Mr. Deane moved towards the door.

"Well, I'm off," he said jauntily. "Sorry we couldn't do business."

"Don't go, Deane."

It was not a request but a quiet command, and in spite of himself the crook stayed exactly where he was. Sir Leo did not go on speaking immediately, and the other man remained uncomfortably, his hand on the doorknob.

The silence lasted for perhaps a minute, and again Mr. Deane attempted to take his leave.

"It's no good, I can't reconsider it," he said. "I've thought it over, and I know what I'm talking about."

"Don't be silly, Deane." Sir Leo's tone was gentle and if anything a trifle bored. "You will move into this hotel tomorrow, and I will make arrangements for the ceremony as soon as possible. You're perfectly all right as long as you don't talk. Get that well into your head."

"Now then, now then, no funny business!" Johnny was becoming impatient. "I'm out of this. Get that into your head."

"I'm afraid you're not." Sir Leo was still leaning back with closed eyes. "I'm afraid you're in this inextricably, Mr. Deane. If you're wise you'll go home and go to bed now, and dream about your future wife, for if you make any foolish attempts to back out of your bargain, or above all, if you so far forget yourself as to have a long heart-to-heart talk with Inspector Blest or any other police officer, then I'm afraid the Yorkshire Constabulary will have to hear the sad story of the wealthy Mr. Emlyn Maughan, which may lead them to make a search of a certain disused stone quarry in the vicinity of that interesting little hamlet, Manchester."

On the last words he opened his eyes and glanced across the room. The change in the unfortunate Major was pitiful. The colour had vanished from his face, and his eyes were round, brown, and terrified, like a beaten dog's.

"I didn't do it," he said. "It wasn't me. I saw him there, but I didn't kill him. On my dying oath I swear it—I—"

"That's all right." Sir Leo cut him short. "Don't distress yourself, my dear fellow. Have a cigar. I have no doubt that you could make a very satisfactory story to the police, one which perhaps you could make them believe, but in case you should not care to go to all that unnecessary bother, why not carry on with our little bargain whereby you will receive an assured annuity of one thousand, payable at twenty pounds a week."

Johnny Deane was a broken man. His lips were still white, and he was trembling.

"All right," he said. "All right. Move into this hotel tomorrow, you said? I'll be here. Good-night, sir."

"Good-night, Deane," said Sir Leo cheerfully, adding, "Don't look so downtrodden, man. You're going to be married."

Sir Leo's Thyn's mood lasted until the Major was well out of the suite. As soon as he was alone, however, it vanished with remarkable suddenness. He sat up, threw away his cigar, and strode up and down the room, his hands thrust deep in his pockets. His forehead was creased and his dark eyes almost hidden by the heavy rolls of flesh above them.

The soft opening of the anteroom door made him turn abruptly.

"Oh, it's you, Marsh, is it?" he said. "Do come in. I want to talk to you."

Saxon Marsh came into the room noiselessly. He was a tall man whose hair had once been red but had now faded to a nondescript colour midway between straw and white.

Perhaps the most startling fact about him was the remarkable thinness of his face. The bones of his skull showed clearly, and his deep-set pale eyes looked as though they were set in a skeleton.

He had been one of Sir Leo's private clients for thirty years, and there were many strange stories told of his curious hermit-like existence. He was reputed to be very rich, but few people actually knew much about him.

He perched himself now on the extreme edge of the formal little sofa which was part of the room's ornate suite and crossed his long thin legs, encased in tight striped trousers.

Sir Leo stood with his back to the window and regarded him.

"The police," he said.

Saxon Marsh nodded. "Yes, Inspector Blest. A personable young officer, very well thought of at the Yard, I believe."

His voice had a curious impersonal note in it, as though he were talking about things that could not possibly concern him.

The other man went on.

"The girl was lying. She met Inspector Blest in the lounge at three o'clock this afternoon. After half-an-hour's conversation they went for a ride in his car. She was returning from this ride when you met her. I inquired discreetly about this and heard it from the commissionaire."

Sir Leo's face darkened. "I guessed that, but I hoped it wasn't true," he said resignedly. "How much did she tell him, do you think?"

Saxon Marsh shrugged his shoulders. "Who knows?" he said. "But one thing she can't have told him, the thing that is really interesting."

Sir Leo looked at him questioningly.

"That the man who marries her before she is twenty-five inherits three hundred thousand pounds," said Saxon Marsh, still in the same odd singsong tone. "She would hardly have told him that, my dear Thyn, because she doesn't know it herself."

Sir Leo swore.

"Why on earth did old Silas Gillimot make such an idiotic will?"

The other man laughed softly. "It has turned out very well for us," he said.

Sir Leo shook his head. "Don't talk about it," he said. "You frighten me. You're such a cold-blooded customer—I'd never have dared to go through with this thing if it hadn't been for you."

It is interesting to record that Saxon Marsh looked slightly flattered by this announcement.

"Not at all," he said. "It was common sense. When we were in great need of a large sum of money and three hundred thousand pounds lay to our hands, it would have been criminal not to use it."

Sir Leo passed his hand through his short white hair.

"How much did we—did we—"

"Use?" suggested Marsh. "It's a prettier word than 'embezzle.' Let me see: to date, about eighty thousand pounds. Nothing to worry about at all. I hope I may be forgiven if I confess that I overheard some of your interview with the Major. I should like to congratulate you on the way you handled him. He'll take his twenty pounds a week and ask no questions. We have only to get them married, and we're safe. Not a pleasant person, the Major, but infinitely preferable to that foolish young Mr.—let me see, what was his name?—Ingleton-Gray."

Sir Leo spun round. "For heaven's sake, be quiet," he said. "It's the same police inspector, you know. He may have followed me down here. I saw he wasn't satisfied at the club."

Saxon Marsh smiled placidly. "I don't think that matters in the least," he said. "Scotland Yard has the disadvantage of requiring cast-iron proof before it interferes with respectable men. In fact," he went on, "the way things have worked out has been really extraordinary. The very eccentricities of the will, the fact that the girl has no capable relations, and the clause which makes you sole trustee, have put the whole thing into our hands."

"I wonder why he made it," said Sir Leo suddenly. "Why leave a fortune to the husband?"

"Silas Gillimot was a very extraordinary man," said Saxon Marsh. "I knew him. He believed that no woman was capable of handling money, and he believed in early marriages. It seemed to him the most natural thing in the world to leave his money to the man Judy Wellington married, if he should marry her without knowing of the fortune before she was twenty-five. Oh yes, Sir Leo, I think we have to congratulate ourselves on the way things are turning out."

"She is twenty-four now," said Sir Leo slowly. "Twenty-four and six months. If the thing hadn't been so imminent I don't know whether I'd have done it."

Saxon Marsh took out a silver cigarette case and drew from it a long scented Turkish cigarette.

"You've done the only thing a sensible man could do," he said. "The only thing you have to fear is something going wrong before she marries. If she reaches her twenty-fifth birthday, remember, the fortune goes..."

Sir Leo nodded and his dark eyes flickered. "Yes," he said. "That must never happen."

Still puffing at his impossible cigarette, Saxon Marsh rose and joined his friend by the window. For some time the two men stood looking at the scintillating scene without. Waves of music came to them, and soft laughter and voices rose up from the floodlighted beach.

Saxon Marsh sighed. "Quite romantic," he said. "Has it ever occurred to you, Sir Leo, that it's very fortunate that the charming Miss Wellington should be such an invalid? The healthy modern young woman is not so easy to manage, and if she once took the bit between her teeth she might give us quite a lot of trouble."

Sir Leo grunted. "There's no point in conjecture of that sort," he said. "The girl is an invalid. I never saw anyone who looked so ill in all my life. There's no doubt about her state of health, Marsh, is there?"

Saxon Marsh threw his cigarette out of the window and watched its shining arc disappear into the shrubbery below.

"I wonder," he said softly. "I wonder."

4

A POLICEMAN'S LOT

INSPECTOR DAVID BLEST was facing the fact that he had fallen as deeply in love as any youngster with his first sweetheart.

The discovery alarmed him considerably, but he did not lose his head. David Blest was a practical young man with practical ambitions and ideas. He realized that the one girl in the world might very well be suspicious of him, since he had not thought to mention his calling to her, though during their brief afternoon together there had seemed quite enough to talk about without discussing his work.

But he also realized that she was in considerable danger of a fatal and, in the circumstances, wholly incomprehensible mésalliance, and it was this aspect of the affair which was engaging his attention at the moment.

A call to Scotland Yard had established one thing: nothing definite was known against Deane at present, and although his name had been mentioned in an inquiry from Yorkshire, nothing further had transpired.

Having drawn a blank, David was on his way to have an

informal and friendly chat with Major Deane at his hotel. That hotel, he had already discovered, was not the Queen's. The Major had not been quite so frank at their meeting on the day before as it had appeared at the time.

Westbourne, although a popular and prosperous seaside town, had not a great variety of hotels. The mammoth Arcadian and its sister, the Queen's, catered for most of the wealthier patrons, and the poorer holiday maker was not encouraged by the townsfolk.

Johnny Deane's choice, therefore, lay between four or five small, select establishments, for David guessed that he would not patronize one of the hundreds of boarding houses and pensions which filled the side streets.

At the moment Inspector Blest was headed for the Empress, which overlooked the Municipal Gardens, just the quiet, respectable place in which the Major would feel most at home. David's jaw set grimly as he anticipated the interview. Inspector Blest had made up his mind: Deane was going to talk.

He paused outside the old-fashioned entrance and bought a paper from a street vendor.

The booking clerk, an aged, bespectacled individual, smiled at his question.

"Major Deane?" he said. "Oh yes, he's staying here. But he's not in yet. See, his keys are still on the board. If you'd sit down in the vestibule there, sir, you'd catch him as he came in."

There seemed nothing else for it, and David settled down on one of the hard plush sofas which lined the mirrored walls. The place was very nearly deserted. Although the Empress was filled to capacity, most of its patrons preferred to take their amusement in the ballroom of the Arcadian and the Queen's, using the Empress merely as a place to eat and sleep.

He had been sitting there for some time, looking out through the wide-open doorway into the street beyond, when he heard his own name uttered in a husky confidential whisper.

He looked up sharply to see an elderly, somewhat lugubrious

individual standing before him. This person had come up softly in enormous rubber-shod boots, and David, catching sight of him, smiled.

Although to the best of his knowledge he had never seen the man before in his life, the type was unmistakable. The red, slightly sad face, the closely cropped grey hair, the heavy figure clad in shiny blue serge, and above all the outrageous boots: the young Inspector would have known him anywhere for what he was, the house detective.

Seeing David smile, the newcomer looked gratified.

"I thought you wouldn't mind me speaking to you, sir," he said, "but I was a sergeant at the Yard once meself—oh, long before your time. But I've still got some old friends there, and I get to know all the new faces. My name's Bloomer," he went on. "Ex-Sergeant Bloomer. I don't suppose you're down here on a case, sir?"

He spoke so wistfully that it was all David could do to hide his amusement.

"Well, no, I'm afraid I'm not, exactly," he said. "I'm on leave."

"Oh, I see." The hope died out of ex-Sergeant Bloomer's eyes, and he sighed. "It's a deadly life," he confessed after a pause. "Nothing ever 'appens down 'ere. I've been down 'ere five years and never had anything more exciting than a case of petty larceny. But I read all about you, sir. That was a smart piece of work, if you'll excuse me saying so, when you caught the Eldorado murderer."

David had no desire to discuss his past exploits, especially at such a time, but in spite of his own troubles he had enough compassion left to sympathize with this sad old watchdog whose great days were over.

It also occurred to him that he might possibly be useful.

"You've got a man staying here called Deane," he said. "Major Deane."

"Oh?" The ex-sergeant looked interested. "Has he been up to

anything? He's leaving tomorrow. Going over to the Arcadian, I heard. I didn't take to him meself. To tell you the truth, I didn't really notice 'im much. Don't tell me," he went on with dismay, "that I've been sitting 'ere all these years waiting for something to 'appen and 'ave missed something going on right under me nose?"

David shook his head. "Don't worry, Sergeant," he said. "He hasn't done anything at all, yet. I just wanted a word with him, that's all."

"I see. I get you, sir." Bloomer looked very knowing. "I'll keep an eye on 'im meself. He should be in at any time now. So *he's* an interesting bird, is he?" he went on thoughtfully. "Well, that's the second. Still, they often turn out to be disappointing," he continued after a pause. "I'm always getting me hopes raised by seeing a familiar face. And then what do I find about 'em? They've been going straight since I left the Force. Not a stain on their characters.

"I'll tell you who we 'ave got 'ere, sir." A certain amount of animation had come into his tone, and he settled himself beside David on the couch. "He only came today. Walked in calm as you please. I don't suppose he thought there was a soul who'd recognize 'im. But I did. I never forget a face."

"Oh?" said David. He was bored by the old man's garrulousness but had not the heart to snub him.

Bloomer lowered his voice and spoke with great solemnity.

"The Fenchurch Street case."

"Eh?" David looked at him in surprise. The words meant nothing to him.

"The Fenchurch Street case," repeated the house detective. "Oh, it was long before your time. It must be twenty years ago. But it made a great stir at the time. Young fellow with a good position in a firm of solicitors, very much the gentleman 'e was, was arrested on a charge of burgling 'is own office. It was evident that the job 'ad bin done from the inside, and it was really a choice between 'im and another fellow. The night watchman was badly hurt, though, and in the end we collared this fellow and 'e went down for seven years.

"Of course, 'e's changed now. That's twenty years ago. It's thirteen years since 'e came out. But I recognized 'im as soon as 'e came in here this morning. Oh, I'd know 'im anywhere. I never forget a face."

"That's interesting," said David, trying hard to sound sincere. "What was his name?"

Bloomer looked crestfallen.

"That's what's worrying me," he said. "I can't remember. I could find out, of course, by looking up the case. But there, it'll come back to me. He calls himself Birch now, Lionel Birch. But that's not right. That wasn't 'is name then. I'm really waiting 'ere to 'ave another good look at 'im. Per'aps when I see 'im again the name'll pop into me 'ead.

"That was always my trouble," he went on with a burst of confidence. "Never forgot a face, but never remembered a name."

He shook his head sadly, and David looked away.

They had been sitting in silence for some moments when ex-Sergeant Bloomer coughed warningly.

"There 'e is, sir," he said in a hoarse whisper. "Just getting out of that taxi outside. See 'im? That soldierly-looking chap with the white 'air. That's the man I've been telling you about. 'E served seven years at Dartmoor. 'E doesn't look it, does 'e?"

David glanced out of the open doorway to see a distinguished-looking man, albeit somewhat shabbily dressed, stepping out of a cab. From where he sat David could see the sharp, piercing eyes and careworn but still aquiline features.

There was something interesting about the face, and he continued to watch the man with idle curiosity.

Instead of paying off the driver, the newcomer gave him some instructions. Then he turned back to the body of the cab and spoke to someone inside.

It was at that moment that a girl leaned out and kissed the old man. The brilliant lights of the hotel sign fell upon her face, and ex-Sergeant Bloomer's hoarse whisper reached David.

"Well!" he said. "Fancy that! At his time of life too."

But Inspector Blest remained where he was, staring before him, blank bewilderment settling down upon him for the second time that day.

For the face of the girl who had leaned out of the taxicab to kiss the distinguished-looking man about whom ex-Sergeant Bloomer had made such interesting revelations was the face of Judy Wellington.

The cab drove away, and the man whom Bloomer had called Lionel Birch advanced slowly down the red-carpeted hall.

After he had assimilated the first shock David watched the newcomer curiously. It was obvious that the man was absorbed in his own thoughts and that they were not altogether pleasant, for he walked slowly, and his eyes were fixed gloomily in front of him.

As he came nearer, David had his first impressions confirmed. The man who now called himself Lionel Birch had at one time been handsome and was still distinguished. It was true that his years in prison had left their mark upon him, but it was evident that, unlike so many men of his class, his spirit had not been broken by the degradation, nor had his innate dignity been entirely destroyed.

When the newcomer was halfway across the hall he stopped abruptly and seemed for the first time to become aware of the small lizard-skin case he carried, for an exclamation of dismay escaped him as he looked down at it.

David followed his glance, and if he had ever entertained any doubts concerning the identity of the girl in the taxi they vanished instantly. The case provided irrefutable proof. It was Judy's. He had seen it on her knee in his own car only that afternoon.

It was quite obvious what had happened: The older man had

been carrying the box for the girl and had inadvertently brought it with him on getting out of the cab, and, since it contained the main ingredients of Judy's "disguise," David could well understand his concern if he shared her secret.

He watched him hurry back to the doorway and glance helplessly down the now empty road. At first it seemed that he would go off in pursuit, but he changed his mind and came back past the two policemen.

"'E's pinched 'er 'andbag," whispered Sergeant Bloomer excitedly. "I wonder—"

David kicked him. "Don't be an ass," he said softly, and Bloomer was silent.

The newcomer had now paused at the reception desk, and from where they sat they could hear his request, put forward in a pleasant, cultured voice which reminded David unaccountably of another voice he had heard lately but which he did not instantly place.

"I've just made a very foolish mistake," Mr. Birch was saying. "A lady gave me a lift back in her cab. I carried this case for her, and, like a complete idiot, I've brought it in with me. She's staying at the Arcadian. Could you send a boy down with it at once?"

The elderly bespectacled soul behind the counter looked faintly shocked.

"It's past ten, sir," he said. "Nearly eleven. I'm afraid I've got no boys on duty now."

He spoke civilly but managed to convey that he regretted the guest's unreasonableness in making such a request rather than his own inability to accommodate him.

A faint touch of colour appeared on the older man's cheek bones.

"But surely there's someone?" he said gently. "You could get me a messenger, perhaps? One of those post office people. I must send this down to the Arcadian immediately. It's most important."

The clerk looked uncomfortable. "I'm afraid there's no one here, sir," he said firmly. "It's very late, you see." He added, glancing meaningly towards the door: "It's a very fine night, sir."

The inference was very clear, and Mr. Birch's colour deepened as in his brown eyes there appeared an inexplicable embarrassment.

"Er—yes," he said. "Yes, it is. But I don't think I'll go myself."

Matters seemed to have come to an impasse. The clerk was anxious to be polite but determined not to be helpful, and the old man stood hesitating.

David rose impulsively. He had come to see Johnny Deane, it was true, but Deane could wait. After all, was there not Bloomer to keep an eye on him? While here, thrust into his very hands, was an opportunity to obtain the one thing that in his heart he wanted most in the world: five minutes' private conversation with Judy, minutes in which to explain.

He stepped forward.

"Excuse me," he said smiling, "but I couldn't help overhearing your difficulty. I'm staying at the Arcadian myself. I came up here for a few minutes' conversation with a friend—" his glance indicated the ex-sergeant, who swelled visibly with pride at the description—" and I'm going back there now. I should be delighted to take anything back for you, if I may."

Birch turned to him. David's voice and appearance were completely convincing, and the older man smiled. His gratitude and relief were quite extraordinary, and in spite of the very questionable introduction he had had to him, David felt a genuine liking for the man.

"That's really extremely kind of you, my dear sir," he said eagerly. "If you wouldn't mind handing this case in at the office at the Arcadian and having it sent up to Miss Judy Wellington, I should be extremely grateful. I'm afraid the poor child may be lost without it."

The quiet, cultured voice again struck a chord in David's memory, but it was so disconcerting to find that the sound of Judy's name on a stranger's lips gave him an altogether unaccountable thrill that he gave the similarity no further thought.

Mr. Birch made him write down the name on the back of an envelope, although the young man could have told him that the chances of his forgetting that name of all names were the most remote in the world.

David took the case and caught a glimpse of the booking clerk looking at him dubiously, and after a moment the man beckoned Bloomer and had a moment's whispered conversation with him.

David was amused. If Mr. Lionel Birch were peculiarly trusting towards total strangers, officials of the Empress Hotel were not so ingenuous.

Bloomer evidently stood surety for him, however, for the clerk seemed satisfied and even favoured him with a gracious nod.

Birch was very grateful and managed to convey to David without ever appearing overeffusive that he was doing him a great service.

Bloomer accompanied the inspector to the door.

"On to something, sir?" he whispered with such childlike eagerness that David had not the heart to disappoint him.

"I don't know, Bloomer," he said darkly. "I don't know. Keep an eye on Deane for me, will you? I shall be back in about an hour or less. I shall hope to have a word with him."

"Right you are, Captain," said Bloomer, permitting himself the familiar form of address. "Right you are. I'll have him all spread out for you."

In a louder tone he said: "Good-night, Mr. Blest. Good-night, sir."

David strode off down the road, clutching the case as though it were his one hope of salvation.

He was so engrossed in his thoughts, so oddly perturbed at the prospect of the interview in front of him, that his usually acute observation failed him for once, and he did not notice the emaciated figure in the black coat who drew into the shadows as he passed and stood for some moments looking after him, a strange expression in his pale, deep-set eyes.

5

WHITE LADY

THE FIRST PERSON David saw as he turned out of the
dark side street and stepped into the flood of light which
bathed the whole of the ornate façade of the Arcadian Hotel was,
curiously enough, the devil himself, complete in crimson tights,
black imperial, and mask.

The fact that he was joined almost immediately by the Queen
of Hearts reminded the startled inspector that the great carnival
ball which he had seen advertised all over the town was taking
place that evening.

The Arcadian was doing its best to live up to its reputation as
the gayest spot on the south coast, and its enormous Louis XV
ballroom was a blaze of light and excitement.

Gay figures in fancy dress thronged the whole of the ground
floor. The big windows leading onto the terrace were thrown
wide, and Harlequins and Columbines, pirates and Anne Boleyns
wandered among the ornamental shrubberies and trod the thick
lawns and the wide stone steps leading down to the sea.

David was grateful for all this excitement downstairs. It gave
him just the opportunity he sought, and with the lizard-skin case
under his arm he set out through the lounge towards the lifts.

Here progress was not quite so easy as he had hoped. The revellers who, earlier in the evening, had kept religiously to the ballroom, had now appropriated the lounge, and the whole place was crowded to suffocation.

Amid such a throng of decorated beauty it was difficult for anyone to make a sensation, but just as David pressed his way among the tables he had an excellent view of one of the minor excitements of the evening.

On the wide staircase which rose up between the two giant lifts, a glistening, ornate structure of white marble and thick red turkey carpet, a woman appeared.

Hers was an unusual beauty, so striking and exotic that even the most disinterested spectator could hardly forbear a second glance at her.

As most of the guests at the Arcadian Carnival were anything but disinterested where beauty was concerned, the newcomer had the satisfaction of a fascinated audience.

The babel of chatter died down for a second before a buzz of excited comment ran round the enormous room.

Even David, whose thoughts were centred on a very different person of a very different type of loveliness, found himself glancing at the woman with interest.

She was not very tall, but she held herself with such arrogant grace that her height appeared to be increased. Nor was she very young. He judged her to be a little over thirty. Her platinum blond hair was waved sleekly against her small head.

Its effect was increased by the dark, provocative eyes, arched with narrow black brows. Her mouth was small and scarlet, and her tiny chin pointed and delicate.

She wore a white dress whose gleaming bodice fitted her incredibly slender body like a second skin and whose enormous skirt swept out round her tiny ankles in a profusion of satin and lace.

In one small hand she carried a little black mask.

She came down the staircase very slowly, obviously enjoying the sensation she was creating.

Old Charlie, the waiter, who had paused beside David, uttered a subdued exclamation as he caught sight of her, and as he turned and recognized David he smiled.

"Still not interested in ladies, sir?" he ventured softly. "She's lovely, isn't she? I never saw anything like her, not in all my born days."

The old man's enthusiasm brought a smile to David's lips.

"Still not very interested," he murmured. "Sorry to disappoint you."

David, who had no desire to make himself conspicuous, waited until the lady in white had completed her leisurely entrance, and then slipped into the lift.

As he stepped out of the lift into the cool wide corridor on the first floor the scene of hectic gaiety which he had just witnessed seemed to belong to another world.

But then so also did the whole day's fantastic business. He was only aware that he was going to speak to Judy, that he was going to hear her voice again, and, if he was lucky, convince her that he was her friend.

Inspector David Blest was a man used to awkward interviews. During the past eight or nine years he had experienced every variety of difficult conversation, or at least, so he had thought until that morning.

Yet now he was conscious of pure apprehension such as he had not felt since his childhood.

The sound of music and occasional laughter floating up on gusts of warm air reached him faintly, but the atmosphere in the corridor was cool and peaceful and remote.

He turned off the main passage and went down the darker corridor where his own and Judy's rooms were situated.

Outside her door he paused, his heart thumping. He had raised his hand to knock when a faint movement down the far end of the passage caught his attention, and he turned and saw her.

She was standing on the little balcony which led up from the hall window and overlooked the terrace below. He was sure it was she. He recognized her petite figure, and the lights from below glinted on her honey-coloured hair.

She looked very small and very pathetic, standing there like a Cinderella peering wistfully down at the dancers in their bright clothes as they passed the open ballroom windows or came out into the dimly lit garden below.

David's shyness vanished and he went forward soberly.

He was almost level with her when she started and swung round. It was with a thrill of delight that he saw the dawning apprehension vanish from her eyes as she recognized him, but her greeting was not encouraging.

"What is it, Inspector Blest?"

The emphasis on "Inspector" was slight, but it was there. David looked at her helplessly.

"I'm sorry about that," he said. "I ought to have told you this afternoon, but I didn't think it mattered."

The girl stiffened. "It doesn't matter," she said. "But I told you very definitely, Inspector, and I hoped that I'd made you understand, although I'm very grateful for your drive this afternoon, our acquaintance cannot possibly continue."

She delivered the formal little speech in a rush and stood very stiff and pale, looking at him coldly.

A wave of despair passed over David.

"I'm sorry," he said lamely. "I only wanted to explain that if I'd known that it would have made any difference either way that I was attached to the police, I should have told you about it at our first meeting. I'm sorry to be so insistent about this, but it was the suggestion that I'd made friends, or at least got to meet you, by false pretences which made me so anxious to put things straight."

The girl turned to him impulsively, her assumed frigidity vanishing in the old disconcerting way which had given him so many tremors earlier in the day.

"I do understand," she said gently. "Really I do. But it isn't only that. You must go away. You mustn't try to see me again. You must leave me alone. Don't you see it's dreadfully important? I can't explain. I would if I could—honestly I would."

She paused, her face raised to his, and it became evident that she found the expression in his eyes disturbing, for she suddenly drew back abruptly and glanced down at the ballroom windows again.

"You mustn't come and look for me like this," she went on without looking at him. "I'm not supposed to be here. It was only that I heard the music and I—well, I just sneaked out to watch for a moment or two before I went to bed. Please go away."

David sighed. "All right," he said wearily. "I'm sorry. As a matter of fact, though, I had a perfectly legitimate excuse for coming up to see you. Here it is. You'll need this, won't you?"

He put the little case into her hand. She stared at it for a moment, and the change in her expression was extraordinary. He heard her catch her breath, but he was completely unprepared for the terror in her voice when she spoke at last.

"Where did you get this?"

The words were uttered in a husky whisper.

"Where did you get it? I thought—"

She broke off and turned wide, horror-stricken grey eyes upon him.

"What are you doing here? What have you found out?"

He did not answer, and she went on with sudden energy:

"I think I understand! I might have known you would try to make friends with me. You're a police officer. This is all part of your work, isn't it? Don't you think it's rather mean? Don't you think it's rather despicable of you? It's all very well to collect evidence—I suppose you've got to—but you needn't go about it quite in this way, need you?"

David's good temper, common sense, and natural restraint suddenly snapped. The bitterness and contempt in her voice was more than he could bear, and moved by a force completely outside himself he caught her by the shoulders.

"Don't talk like that," he said, his voice unnaturally calm. "You're making an absurd mistake. That case was given me by a stranger whom I met at the Empress Hotel. He tried to get a boy to bring it over to you, and I heard his request refused. It was such a wonderful opportunity to get a word with you that I jumped at it. I told him I was coming back and asked if I could bring it along.

"My dear girl," he went on earnestly, his eyes on her own, "don't you see I don't care what sort of mess you're in? I want to help you. You've got to let me help if I can."

The girl was standing very still. Her face was pale in the faint light, and he saw her wide grey eyes staring at him with something more than mere surprise in their depths.

After he had finished speaking he stood where he was, looking down at her. He was breathless and very sincere.

Judy sighed. It was the ghost of a sound and barely reached him.

"Oh, I believe you," she said simply.

He bent towards her, but she pushed him away gently.

"Oh please," she said. "Please go away. It's no use. Don't you see it's no use?"

Her voice was trembling, and he could feel her hand quiver as she touched his sleeve.

David pulled himself together and became at least a semblance of his old practical self.

"Look here," he said, "you've got to let me help you. For heaven's sake, don't be afraid of me. I wouldn't do anything to hurt you for the world. But I can't stand aside and see you mixed up in this extraordinary business without doing something. There is one thing I've got to know. Who is the man who gave me this bag? Who is the man whom you took to the Empress Hotel in a cab less than half an hour ago?"

She shot him a startled glance, some of her old terror returning.

"You know that?" she said.

He nodded. "Yes, I saw you. Who is Lionel Birch, Judy?"

She looked at him searchingly. "I don't know why I trust you," she said suddenly, "but I do. Lionel Birch is my uncle—Uncle Jim. He's no relation really, but he brought me up and has looked after me nearly all my life, and I am very fond of him. My mother died before I can remember, and then for a time I think I had a nurse, but after I was five years old I went down to the country to live with Uncle Jim. He's been so kind to me. He educated me, taught me everything I know, and until—well, until three weeks ago he managed to keep me down there away from my guardian."

A light of understanding broke over David.

"Is that the reason for your extraordinary disguise?" he said.

She nodded. "Yes. It started years ago when Sir Leo wanted to take me away from Uncle Jim. We hit on this scheme. Whenever Sir Leo came down I was too ill to be moved and taken to London to live. Gradually he got to believe that I was a helpless invalid. Then, three weeks ago, he put his foot down, and I had to promise to meet him here, ill or not. Now you understand everything."

David took her hands.

"Why do you have to obey Sir Leo so implicitly?" he asked. "Is that because of Uncle Jim too?"

She nodded. "Don't ask me about it," she said. "Please. I ought not to have told you so much. You can't help me. You can't do anything. You—"

She stopped abruptly. Someone was coming down the passage. The girl clutched his arm.

"Sir Leo mustn't know Uncle Jim followed me to Westbourne, and he mustn't see you with me," she whispered, panic-stricken.

David stepped back into the shadow made by the curtain and drew the girl in beside him. His movement had been as silent as a cat's, and he was convinced that they were unnoticed.

The footsteps came closer, and Judy heaved a sigh of relief as she heard the click of high-heeled shoes. Whoever the newcomer might be, it was certainly not Sir Leo.

The footsteps ceased, and the young people peered out of their hiding place to catch a glimpse of the stranger. What David saw was not the least surprising thing in a surprising day.

Standing before Judy's own door, her ear against the panel, was the woman who had made a sensational entrance into the lounge such a short while before.

He recognized her instantly, of course. It would have been impossible not to do so, since her appearance was unforgettable.

Having listened in silence for some moments, the woman raised her hand and, glancing furtively down the corridor, tapped softly on the wood.

Receiving no response, she opened the white evening bag she carried and extracted a key. She had just fitted it in the lock when Judy touched David's arm.

"I've never seen her before in my life," she whispered. "What's she doing there?" Moved by a common impulse they both stepped forward.

It was Judy who spoke.

"Can I help you?" she said quietly. "That's my door."

The woman started back, and just for a moment a flicker of alarm crept into her eyes. But it was only for a moment, and David found himself admiring the extraordinary aplomb with which she carried off a very awkward situation.

"Oh, is it?" she said. "I'm *so* sorry. I only arrived this afternoon, and I'm afraid I must have got confused. Perhaps my room is a *hundred* and forty-nine. I really can't remember. I must go down and inquire."

It occurred to David that he could have pointed out that the number of her room would be stamped upon her key had she not been attempting to open the door with an entirely different sort of implement from any used in the hotel.

As though she feared he might put some such question, the woman hurriedly slipped the key back in her bag and stood surveying them.

Somewhat to their surprise, she did not show any inclination to hurry away. On the contrary, she seemed inclined to stay and chat.

David was puzzled. This was no ordinary type of hotel thief, but even if she had belonged to that particular sisterhood, why on earth should she pick on Judy's room?—Judy, the one person in the hotel, probably, who was supposed by everyone to be in bed asleep?

"I suppose you've been watching the dancing?" The woman glanced towards the window. "It's great fun downstairs. Why aren't you two young people joining in?"

The question was put without direct impertinence, and had it not been for the shrewd, intelligent gleam in the dark eyes David would have put it down as a desire to pass off an awkward moment.

But after seeing those eyes he knew that here was a woman who was not troubled by shyness or gaucherie.

"You really ought to be dancing," she went on, looking at Judy.

She looked very charming, standing there in her billowy white gown, and Judy seemed to respond to her friendliness.

"I—I'm an invalid," she said. "I don't dance."

"An invalid? You poor child!" The sympathy was extraordinarily well done, and David's curiosity increased.

The newcomer eyed him covertly.

"Are you two brother and sister?" she demanded unexpectedly. "You're awfully alike."

This suggestion was so obviously unlikely that David wondered at her daring to try so audacious an opening.

Again it was Judy who answered.

"Oh no, no relation at all."

In spite of herself the vehemence in her tone was noticeable, and the other woman made the most of it. She laughed.

"Oh, I see," she said. "Just friends. Well, I must go downstairs to interview the office and try to discover where my room is. Are you coming?"

She spoke as though she had known them for years, and Judy, like most ingenuous people, responded by replying in the same strain.

"Oh no," she said. "I'm supposed to be in bed. Good-night."

"My name is Marguerite Ferney," the woman murmured.

Again Judy responded.

"I'm Judy Wellington," she said. "Good-night, Miss Ferney."

Already she had opened the door, and it was only as she stepped inside that she smiled back at the man.

"Good-night, David," she whispered, and disappeared.

In spite of his intense curiosity concerning the woman's possible motives in forcing an acquaintance with them, David was conscious of a definite state of disappointment as the door closed.

He turned away and caught Miss Ferney looking at him quizzically; he had the uncomfortable feeling that she had read his thoughts and might, if he were not very careful, chip him about them.

However, she was much more politic.

"We'll go down, shall we?" she suggested, adding inconsequentially, "What a charming girl!"

David did not reply save by the most noncommittal of nods, but he walked down the corridor beside the woman, and they stepped into the lift together.

On closer inspection Marguerite Ferney was an even more interesting person than she had appeared at first sight. David thought he had a pretty thorough knowledge of this particular type of woman. He came up against it fairly often in his work. But never before had he seen so exotic and artificial a specimen with such extraordinarily intelligent eyes; eyes so shrewd and clever that they completely belied the ingenuous, rather vapid, well-meaning character she was endeavouring to assume.

As they rode down together she chattered on in the frankest and most brainless fashion, but all the time David was asking himself what she had been doing at Judy's door and trying to reconcile reason with his conviction that the woman had achieved her purpose, and that that purpose had been nothing more or less than an attempt to strike up an acquaintance, however slight, with Judy Wellington.

He was reproaching himself for being unduly nervous where Judy was concerned when a very curious thing happened.

As they stepped out of the lift together, the woman still talking and smiling up into his face, the first person to see them was Sir Leo.

He had been waiting for the lift to descend and had come forward as the steel doors swung back. David saw his face. He saw the expression change as Sir Leo caught sight of Marguerite Ferney, saw the look that was half fury, half apprehension in his eyes, and then, as his gaze travelled on and he recognized the inspector himself and realized that the two were not only acquainted but seemed to be on the best of terms, the colour slowly drained out of his florid face, and his eyes widened with something which, to the bewildered detective, appeared to be nothing less than frank, unadulterated terror.

Sir Leo stepped hurriedly into the lift as though fearful of being seen and disappeared from view.

Still pondering on this odd incident, David escorted the fascinating Miss Ferney to the office and then left her, firmly refusing to understand her obvious overtures.

He was hurrying back through the lounge when the hoarse voice of the page boy crying his room number caught his attention. He beckoned the youngster and gave his name.

"Mr. Blest, sir?" The boy seemed relieved. "You're wanted on the phone. It seems to be urgent. This way, sir."

David followed the page to the telephone and raised the receiver. Ex-Sergeant Bloomer's voice, hoarse with excitement, reached him across the wire.

"Is that you, Captain? I've been trying to get you for some minutes. Yes, it's urgent all right. It's that fellow Deane you told me to keep an eye on. We've just found him up in his room, shot through the head."

There was a pause as David put a question.

"Yes, sir. Sorry, sir. Quite dead." Bloomer sounded apologetic. "We've sent for the local police, of course. But I thought I'd let you in on the ground floor."

"Right, Bloomer. I'll be over right away."

Slowly David hung up the receiver and for a moment stood staring unseeingly at the instrument.

The page, who had hung about outside the booth, sensing a sensation, mentally decided that the gentleman had received bad news, but his youthful mind had no conception of the utter chagrin and dismay which at that moment descended upon Inspector David Blest.

Dead. Johnny Deane dead. The one witness upon whom he had relied to give him the all-important information he sought. David could hardly believe it. Five minutes before he had been confident that the whole of the bewildering mystery which surrounded Judy Wellington would be made clear to him.

Then Sir Leo, the beautiful Marguerite Ferney, and the strange, likable figure of Lionel Birch had all seemed to him to be parts of a puzzle to which he held the key.

Now, in one single moment, that key had been torn from his hand, and he was plunged into a darkness more abysmal than ever.

He found it in his heart to be sorry for Johnny Deane, that ineffectual, good-tempered little crook who had never done anything, so far as David knew, to merit sudden death. Now he had been struck down callously so that he might not betray a secret. That secret, David reflected, must be even more important to someone than he had at first supposed.

He walked out of the booth and made his way slowly across the lounge. As he went he cursed himself bitterly for several kinds of a fool. Had he not been so ridiculously anxious to have a word with Judy he would have let Lionel Birch get the lizard-skin case back to the girl in his own way and would have waited for Johnny Deane as he had intended.

It suddenly occurred to him that he was taking it for granted that the man had been murdered, Bloomer had not said so. It might even be suicide, and in that case the whole business was inexplicable.

As it was, David, who entertained the gravest suspicions of Sir Leo where the death of Ingleton-Gray was concerned, could not see the baronet as a possible killer of Deane. The two had seemed on the best of terms six or seven hours before, and, at any rate, he had just seen Sir Leo get into the lift, and, presuming that Bloomer had rung him immediately the crime was committed, the older man had not had much chance to get back from the Empress to the Arcadian in so short a time.

He was lucky to find a taxi outside the hotel and a few seconds later was being whirled away to the scene of the tragedy. He sat forward in the cab, his arms clasping his knees. He was worried. His own position, he foresaw, might be very difficult. He was out of his district, and the local police are often jealous of Scotland Yard and are by no means always anxious to solicit their help.

However, he reflected philosophically, the only thing to do was to go and find out, and accordingly he sat where he was, watching impatiently the darkened houses flicker by as their blank window-panes reflected the lights of the cab.

When he arrived the Empress gave every appearance of being closed. There was not very much light in the hall, and only a small opening in the iron trellis-work doors at the foot of the front steps betrayed that something unusual was afoot.

David pushed his way in and strolled into the foyer. There were two uniformed policemen conversing softly at the far end, and one of them came towards him and would have spoken had not Bloomer hurried out of the porter's room and forestalled the man.

The old sergeant looked a good ten years younger. However disastrous the tragedy might be for the hotel, however tragic the effect upon the unfortunate Major, it had certainly done old Bloomer a world of good.

There was a flicker of excitement in his eyes, and he looked, David was shocked to see, supremely happy.

His opening remark bore out this impression.

"It's like old times, isn't it, Captain?" he said. "Oh, it's a murder all right. I found the poor chap meself. He came in just after you left and went straight up to 'is room. I hung about for half an hour or so, and then I just wandered up there casual-like to see that 'e was all right. There was a light under 'is door, and I thought I might as well look in. I knocked and got no reply, knocked again, and finally got the chambermaid to open the door with 'er pass-key.

"I sent 'er in with an extra blanket, you see," he added knowingly. "Well, she let out a scream which you could have heard at the other end of the town, and I rushed in.

"There 'e was, lying across the bed, a nice neat hole through 'is forehead.

"Stop," he went on, as David opened his mouth. "I know what

you're going to ask me, Captain, and I can answer in one. There wasn't. There wasn't a gun about anywhere."

He paused for breath and grinned at David.

"Murder," he said at last, a certain amount of frankly ghoulish satisfaction in his tone. "After all these years, with nothing ever happening, a murder! I don't mind telling you, Captain, I've got a theory already, but I'm not spilling it in case I'm wrong."

"Who's in charge of the case?" said David more brusquely than he had intended.

"Inspector Winn, of the local C.I.D. Detective Inspector Winn."

A certain lack of enthusiasm in Bloomer's tone indicated that the old ex-sergeant had not much use for the gentleman in question.

"However, you go right upstairs, sir," he went on. "It's room seventy-three, on the second floor. I can't come with you because—" he lowered his voice—"between you and me, I think the chief constable 'imself's coming down, and I've got to be here to take 'im straight up to the manager. Colonel Cream: he is a very nice gentleman."

"All right." David moved towards the staircase. He was the last man in the world to go butting in on another's preserves, but in this particular case he felt he had a very great personal interest.

Bloomer hurried after him.

"It's the second floor, sir," he said. "If you hear a bit of excitement on the first that's just the manager. 'E's taken the thing to heart terribly. O' course it's bad for 'im, you see, right in the middle of the season."

David shook off the sergeant and hurried up the staircase. Bloomer was not without charm, but there were times when he got on David's nerves, and this was one of them.

He did notice on the first floor a certain amount of quiet hubbub. A distraught-looking young man with "private secretary" written all over him hurried out of a door marked "Office" and disappeared down the corridor, a sheaf of papers on his arm.

David pressed on.

Like many hotels of its type, the Empress was something of a sham inasmuch as its first floor was less luxurious than its ground floor, and the second floor less magnificent still.

Treading softly, David made his way down the dimly lit passage, noting the numbers on the doors. He found number seventy-three without much difficulty and paused a moment before going in. Indeed, this was necessary, for a policeman in uniform stood on duty before the door.

To this somewhat wooden-faced individual David gave his name and rank. The magic words "Scotland Yard" had an instantaneous effect. The man looked at him respectfully.

"If you'll just wait a minute, I'll tell the inspector you're here, sir," he said. "I can't show you straight in, because I've had orders to keep everybody out."

David smiled. "That's all right, Constable," he said. "Orders are orders, I know that."

The policeman looked relieved and, stepping deferentially, slipped inside the room, closing the door after him.

In three minutes he was out again. He was very red, and his round uncomfortable face shone with embarrassment.

"I'm very sorry, sir," he said, breathing heavily, "but Inspector Winn says he's very busy just now, and if you have anything to say pertinent to the case he will interview you with the rest of the witnesses downstairs in the lounge in about an hour."

David reddened. He had felt that there might be opposition to his taking a hand in the case, but he had not expected quite such flagrant rudeness. The constable looked positively wretched.

"I'm very sorry, sir," he repeated. "Very sorry." His voice trailed away into silence.

"Please go back and tell Inspector Winn that I think I can identify his man for him," said David.

Again the constable disappeared, looking even more wretched than before.

This time he did not return. Instead, the door was thrown open, and a dark military figure in an inspector's uniform strode out into the corridor.

Inspector Winn only just attained regulation height, but he made up for his lack of inches with a tremendous self-sufficiency. His small dark eyes were angry, and the points of his small black moustache positively bristled.

"Inspector Blest of Scotland Yard?"

David nodded. "That is my name, and I came to offer you any assistance I could. I think that if you have not already identified the dead man I can do that for you."

"That's very kind of you." There was a sneer in the other man's voice. "But I assure you, you're being overzealous. We can manage a little thing like this without any help from Scotland Yard."

David stared at the man and suddenly decided that he was overwrought. The importance of the case had gone to his head, and he did not fully realize the effect of what he was saying.

David stiffened. "I beg your pardon, Inspector," he said. "I assure you I had no wish to intrude." Then, turning on his heel, he strode off down the corridor, his body held a trifle more erect even than usual and his eyes flashing.

He was still angry when he reached the lounge again. The lift, of course, was not working at so late an hour, and he could see down into the hall for some time before he actually reached it.

Standing directly in his way were old Bloomer and a white-haired old gentleman who David knew instinctively must be Colonel Cream, the chief constable for the district.

The Colonel was a plump, affable individual with an expansive smile and a pair of the most enormous white moustaches David had ever seen.

Bloomer said something as David approached, and the Colonel swung round.

"Inspector Blest? Really? God bless my soul, this is a fortunate coincidence. My dear young sir, allow me to introduce myself. My name's Cream, J. Pennyfield Cream, chief constable for the district. Bloomer here tells me you already know about our difficulty. I'm delighted to meet you, delighted."

He was effusive but so obviously sincere in his delight that David's anger evaporated.

The Colonel went on talking. David found afterwards that this was one of his peculiarities: he always talked, whether anyone else had anything important to say or not.

"This really is a blessing," the Colonel continued. "The best man at the Yard right on the scene of the crime half an hour after it's happened. That's the kind of organization I like to see, the organization of Providence. We must have you on this and get it all cleared up. Can't have things happening like this right in the middle of the season, just when all these poor fellows are trying to put by a little for the winter. This is splendid! You must get down to it at once."

David hesitated. He was in a very awkward situation. The old man's enthusiasm was irresistible, however.

"Apart from the poor fellow who's been killed," he was saying, "there are the living to think of. This is the second murder case I've ever had since I've been chief constable. I was six weeks late calling in the Yard last time, and I've never heard the end of it. And I'm not going to make that mistake again. You're not on a case now, are you?"

"No, sir. I'm on leave."

"Splendid. They must make it up to you. I'll get on to Sir Gervase and fix it all up. Meanwhile, you must get to work."

David drew back. "I don't think Inspector Winn—" he began.

The Colonel's small bright blue eyes flickered uncertainly for a moment.

"Winn'll be delighted," he said. "Winn's a good man, one of the best we've got. But he hasn't had the experience. We don't get a murder every day at Westbourne. What we need is a man who's handled the same sort of thing before. Come along, my dear fellow. I suppose there's no chance of these lifts working, Bloomer? No? Well, come along. We must go by the stairs."

Once again David climbed up to the second floor of the Empress Hotel.

They entered room seventy-three, and Colonel Cream, either unaware of any friction between the two men or else magnificently disregarding it, reintroduced them and, in the pontifical way of chief constables, bade them make haste with their arrest.

After some considerable talk about the case, when all the facts David already knew were repeated, the Colonel turned to the local police officer.

"You're extremely lucky, Winn," he said. "Here we have one of the best men at the Yard arriving at the precise moment that you need him. Now I shall leave you to it. Put Inspector Blest in full possession of the facts and then, for heaven's sake, put your heads together and get this thing cleared up quickly. I'm going down to see the manager. Bloomer wanted to take me straight to him, but I thought I'd see you two first.

"Meanwhile I'll phone the Yard and make the necessary arrangements about Inspector Blest. Don't worry, my boy," he went on, as David glanced at him despairingly—the Colonel had been anything but tactful, "don't worry. I assume full responsibility for this. Let me know any new developments, Winn. I shall look in before I go, but, if I forgot to mention it, the phone's by my bed, and you can get me the moment you want me. Goodnight, good-night."

He went out, closing the door firmly behind him. The click of the latch echoed through the disordered and tragic little room.

David Blest turned slowly and surveyed the other man, who he saw to his acute embarrassment was white with anger.

"I'm extremely sorry about all this," he began, "but Colonel Cream collared me on the staircase, and I couldn't very well get out of it."

Inspector Winn's expression did not relax.

"I've been on the Force for twenty years," he said, "and I am not used to taking advice from my juniors. However, if the great resources of Scotland Yard can assist me to solve this very simple little case, I assure you I shall give them the gratitude they deserve."

David said nothing, but his lazy blue eyes had assumed their old sleepiness. The case certainly promised to have its difficulties.

6

THE FRIGHTENED MAN

MARSH, YOU'RE INHUMAN. Either inhuman or you don't realize. You're mad. Good God, man, don't you understand? I tell you I've seen her."

Sir Leo, his shortly cropped white hair standing on end, and his face, which was usually so florid, an unpleasant shade of pinkish grey, strode up and down the thickly carpeted bedroom at the Arcadian, his hands thrust deep in his pockets and his small dark eyes flickering nervously.

There was a soft laugh from the bed. Propped up among the pillows, Saxon Marsh looked even less attractive than he did in the ordinary way. The bed on which he lay was huge, one of the best the Arcadian possessed. Behind the headboard hung a piece of tapestry, forming a canopy, adding considerably to its imposing appearance.

Saxon Marsh's head and shoulders were supported by some half-dozen pillows, and his hands were folded neatly on the coverlet.

"Forgive me," he said, "but you're amusing. Stop in front of the mirror and have a look at yourself. You'll see what I mean."

Sir Leo advanced towards the end of the bed. His state of alarm was pitiable. He was too terrified even to be angry.

"Marsh," he said, "I'm frightened. I'm deeper in this thing than you know. I don't often lose my nerve. I never remember losing it before. But, good God, man, consider my position!"

Saxon Marsh's thin eyelids dropped over his eyes. He looked a trifle bored.

"And I?" he said. "My dear fellow, I'm as deeply concerned in this business as you are, and I'm not alarmed in the least. We've had one or two little setbacks, I admit that, but in any undertaking which involves so much of what perhaps I may call delicate business, these small hitches are only to be expected. If we are very careful and play our part properly I don't think that anything can possibly go wrong. Go to bed, Sir Leo. Go to bed and sleep, as I shall as soon as you leave me alone."

"Small hitches!" exploded Sir Leo. "Haven't I just told you that I saw Marguerite Ferney in this hotel? Do you understand what I'm saying? I tell you I've seen Marguerite Ferney smiling at that young Scotland Yard man and chatting away as though she had known him all her life."

Saxon Marsh remained unimpressed.

"A pretty woman," he observed after a pause. "A very decorative type."

"A dangerous woman," snapped Sir Leo. "Dangerous and clever. We're up against it. My God, if I could get out of this I would!"

The pale eyes of the man in the bed opened and, for the first time since the beginning of the interview, a shrewd expression crept into their depths. Saxon Marsh frowned.

"Pull yourself together, Thyn," he snapped. "What's there to be afraid of in a woman, however many silly policemen she has in tow? There are times when you irritate me. We're men of the world, not to be bothered by small fry."

Sir Leo attempted a laugh and failed miserably.

"Marguerite Ferney is not my idea of small fry," he said. "Once she gets hold of the girl—"

"She won't get hold of the girl," said Marsh quickly. "So don't think about it. It's out of the question. I will look after the girl."

Sir Leo dropped into an armchair and passed his handkerchief over his forehead.

"Too many things," he said huskily, "too many things have gone wrong today. There's that man Deane. He's not safe. I frightened him, but you never know with those fellows. You never know when they're going to lose their nerve completely and run howling to the police. After all, suppose he told his version of the affair? Suppose he went to the police and told them everything and forced my hand? He knows I've no real evidence about that north country business. After all, what's a trial to him if he gets off at the end of it? But with me it's different. The least breath of suspicion and I'm done."

Saxon Marsh yawned and, stretching out his hand, switched off the reading light, which was shining in his eyes.

"I don't think you need bother about Major Johnny Deane any more, Thyn," he said. "He wasn't really a suitable person, you know. You need, if I may say so, more of a man of the world and less of a jailbird. I'll see what I can do. We still have a month or two."

Something in his tone sent an added chill down Sir Leo's spine. The blood rushed into his face and rushed out again.

"What do you mean?" he said hoarsely.

He was sitting in his chair, striving to pierce the gloom which had fallen over the far end of the bed.

"I say don't worry about Deane." Saxon Marsh's voice was even more languorous than before.

"Why?"

The whisper was so soft that it sounded no more than a sigh in the big room.

"Johnny Deane," said Saxon Marsh placidly, "is dead, poor

fellow. He was shot through the head at about a quarter-past eleven this evening. It's very sad, but I don't think he has any relatives to mourn him."

"*What have you done?*"

The four words were uttered in a small, thin voice which Sir Leo would never have recognized as his own. "Oh, my God, what have you done?"

Saxon Marsh sat up in bed.

"Taken a leaf out of your book," he said. "Imitation is the sincerest form of flattery, Sir Leo."

"Imitation?" Thyn was pitiful to see. He moistened his dry lips. "On that occasion the method was foolproof," he muttered. "The place was perfect. But this—this is murder. Obvious murder."

"Quite," said Saxon Marsh, still in the same quiet, satisfied tone. "But neither you nor I know anything about that, Thyn. No possible breath of suspicion can touch us."

"How do you know?" As though he had been turned to ice, Sir Leo sat rigid; yet there were beads of perspiration on his forehead.

"You'll see," promised Saxon Marsh. "You'll see. And now, my friend, for heaven's sake, go to bed. Go to bed and sleep."

Sir Leo peered into the dusk with haggard eyes.

"Sleep?" he muttered incredulously.

"Certainly," said Saxon Marsh placidly. "Why not?"

7

EX-SERGEANT BLOOMER REMEMBERS

I F YOU KNOW so much about the dead man, Inspector Blest, perhaps you would oblige me by explaining who killed him. Then we could all go home."

Inspector Winn allowed the words to be forced out of him against his better judgment. It was three o'clock in the morning, and the two police officers had paused in their labours to drink a cup of coffee sent in to them by a distracted but hopeful manager.

Much careful questioning had revealed nothing. Johnny Deane had walked into the Empress, collected his key from the desk, and had gone up to his room. Apparently no one had seen him alive again.

To make matters worse, Inspector Winn had lost his temper not once but many times, and each time it had made him feel more foolish than before.

After disliking him intensely for the first half hour, David had grown rather sorry for him. The man had ability, but he was alarmed at the size of the task in front of him. A mysterious murder in the middle of the season, with the chief constable himself on the warpath and Scotland Yard called in, was certain to have a great deal of publicity, and Winn was very conscious of his responsibility.

The two men had left the bedroom and were now established in a small office on the ground floor, where they had already questioned some twenty-five witnesses, none of whom had told them anything of any real worth.

David lit his pipe and perched himself on the edge of the table, his arms folded.

"Something'll turn up," he said.

Inspector Winn opened his mouth to speak, but as though in direct fulfilment of David's prophecy, both men were startled by a timid rap on the door.

Winn leapt forward to open it, and a dishevelled figure in a coarse red dressing gown stepped into the room, blinking in the strong light.

David recognized the girl as one of the many chambermaids whom they had already interviewed. She was an ugly girl, coarse-featured and stupid-looking, and had appeared very hysterical at the first interview.

"What is it?" Winn inquired. "You're Miss Dartle, aren't you? Ruth Dartle?"

Miss Dartle burst into tears.

"Edith made me come," she said. "Edith does rooms sixty to eighty. She said I'd got to come and tell you or you'd arrest me."

David and Inspector Winn exchanged glances, and for the first time the younger man saw a gleam of humour and humanity in the local man's black eyes.

"Oh, well, Edith's to blame, is she?" said Winn with a good-natured friendliness which David himself could not have surpassed. "What have you been up to?"

"Oh, I haven't done anything, sir." Miss Dartle wept afresh. "I didn't mean not to tell you. I just forgot. It only came into my head half an hour ago, and me and Edith have been talking about it ever since. She shares a room with me, you see. I would have

72

remembered, but it was such an ordinary thing for a guest to ask me to direct him to a friend's room that I just told him, and it slipped out of my mind."

"What's that?" Both inspectors sat up with the first interest they had shown in Miss Dartle's narrative, and she, feeling that she was a success, gained confidence and became more lucid.

"It was the nice old gentleman in number fifty," she said. "He only came today, but I remember his name quite well, because when I went in to turn down the bed there was his case lying open, and when I shut it I read the name on the label. Mr. Lionel Birch."

David stopped her.

"Let's get this thing straight," he said. "Who asked you the way to whose room?"

"Mr. Birch did, sir. Mr. Birch asked me what room his friend Major Deane slept in, and I told him."

Inspector Winn was scribbling in his notebook.

"When was this?" he said.

"I'm not quite sure, sir. About eleven o'clock tonight, I should say. He was in a great hurry. I thought he wanted to see Major Deane before he went to bed."

Miss Dartle's sense of her own importance increased considerably in the next fifteen minutes. Never before had any two gentlemen shown such interest in her doings, sayings, and impressions in all her life.

But this thrilling experience was cut short by an even greater sensation. One of the plainclothes men on duty in the hall put his head round the door and, after a glimpse of his expression, Winn dismissed the girl, bidding her come to him in the morning, and beckoned the newcomer in.

That worthy in turn motioned peremptorily to someone who stood behind him, and there presently appeared a smart uniformed constable carrying something carefully in a large white handkerchief.

That something proved to be, on closer inspection, a small, slightly battered revolver.

For the first time both inspectors experienced a real thrill of hope. Perhaps, after all, the impossible, incomprehensible business was going to be less difficult than it had at first appeared.

David stretched out his hand but remembered himself in time and gave way to Inspector Winn, who, strangely enough, seemed to appreciate the courtesy.

Taking out his own handkerchief, the elder man picked up the little weapon, being careful not to obliterate any fingerprints.

"I do believe this is it," he said. "Don't you think so, Blest? It's the right calibre, anyway. Where did you find it, Constable?"

"In White Horse Alley, sir. That's the little street that runs along the back of the hotel. It was lying in the road just outside the main service entrance. Of course, I couldn't say how long it would have been there. I've passed down the alley twice tonight already, but I might easily have missed it. It was lying right in the shadow of the houses opposite."

David bent forward and silently indicated the little bright patches on the metal.

"Looks as though it's been dropped from a height," he suggested.

Winn looked at him sharply. Every trace of his old animosity had vanished in his enthusiasm.

"It does, doesn't it?" he said. "Now I wonder."

He walked over to the desk and looked at the plan of the hotel with which the management had furnished him earlier in the evening.

"Rooms twenty, twenty-two and twenty-four on the first floor," he said. "And on the second, forty-six, forty-eight, and—yes, fifty. What did the girl say the fellow's name was?—Lionel Birch. We must have a chat with this Lionel Birch."

David was silent, his brows knitted and his eyes darker than usual and introspective. He was remembering another case not so very long ago, a case when a key had been found under a window, and on that occasion its evidence had been, in David's own opinion, curiously misleading.

After all, if a key, why not a revolver?

This was no time, however, to mention any doubts to Inspector Winn. That gentleman was frankly delighted.

"Lionel Birch," he said. "I'll come out with you, Constable, and see exactly where you found the gun, and then I'll verify this plan, Blest. Anything known about this man Lionel Birch? We'll have him up and put him through it as soon as I've completed the routine."

David said nothing, but he knew that even the impetuous Inspector Winn would hardly drag a man from his bed at four o'clock in the morning unless he was pretty sure in his own mind that the evidence he had collected, or was about to collect, was sufficient for an arrest.

Winn, the plainclothes man, and the constable hurried out to inspect the alley where the gun had been found, and David was left alone. He stood for a moment staring down at the table, a frown gathering upon his brow.

There was something he did not like about the way the case was going, something he could not understand. If the gun had not been found under the window it might have been different, and yet, from his own private knowledge, Lionel Birch was a friend of Judy Wellington's, and who, save a friend of Judy Wellington's, would be likely to want Johnny Deane out of the way so intensely that he stooped to murder?

A friend. After all, the man was more than a friend. He had brought the girl up from childhood. Yet he was no relation. Surely the tie was not strong enough to make that mild-looking old gentleman shoot the little confidence trickster in cold blood?

He paused. The door had opened, and he glanced up, expecting to see Winn return. However, his visitor was a very different person.

Bloomer, his collar loosened and his feet encased in enormous carpet slippers, was standing on the threshold, his small eyes sparkling with excitement.

"I've been turning over me old notebooks," he said without preamble. "I 'ad to come down on the off-chance of finding you alone. I've remembered it, Captain."

David looked at him blankly. His mind was still very far away.

"Remembered what?" he said at last. "I'm sorry, Bloomer, but I don't quite follow you."

"Why, the fellow's name in the Fenchurch Street case." Bloomer looked hurt. "You remember. I was telling you about 'im in the hall this evening. The fellow who was staying here under the name of Birch. The fellow who did seven years at Dartmoor."

He came farther into the room and dropped his voice to a confidential whisper.

"I thought of 'im the moment this business broke, and I went and dug up my old books. I've remembered it all now: the young wife dying and leaving the kid, and all the excitement in the news-papers. It all come back to me."

David stared at the old man in silent fascination. Something warned him of the revelation to come; nevertheless, his heart missed a beat as ex-Sergeant Bloomer's hoarse whisper filled the room.

"His name was Wellington," he said. "Jim Wellington. Does that convey anything to you, Captain? His wife died while he was in jail, and someone looked after the kid—I forget who. It was a girl, as far as I can remember."

Lionel Birch, suspected of killing Major Johnny Deane, was Judy's father!

"It's a wonderful thing, memory is," remarked ex-Sergeant Bloomer affably after what seemed to David to be an interminable pause. "It was lucky I was able to set eyes on 'im for you, wasn't it? It's training that counts every time; every time, that's what I always say."

David looked at the other man sharply. Bloomer's heavy face was positively glistening, and his small eyes danced. He was evidently more than ordinarily elated, and it occurred to the inspector that the house detective might very possibly have been indulging in a hasty celebration at the expense of the house whisky.

However, he was in no mood to think about the old man just then. The staggering quality of the revelation, together with its possible consequences, kept his mind fully occupied.

His immediate inclination was to resign from the case at once, but on second thoughts it occurred to him that there were definite disadvantages in this course of action. Instead of letting Judy out of the business he might be the actual means of dragging her into it.

He sighed. Anyhow, he had plenty of time to think. He could do nothing either way until the morning, when he would see Colonel Cream again.

"These local men!" said Bloomer with contempt. "It's a funny thing, Captain, but they don't seem to have the Yard's flair, do they? This chap Winn, now. He's a sound enough man in 'is way. All right for small cases and such-like. But a thing like this throws 'im off 'is balance."

David frowned. He realized that Bloomer was flouting etiquette to a disgraceful extent by permitting himself to speak of one inspector in such terms in front of a colleague.

He had opened his mouth to remonstrate when the door opened and the subject of Bloomer's remarks returned.

As soon as he caught sight of him David's qualms returned. Inspector Winn was flushed and excited. The discovery of the gun had sent his hopes soaring, and all his old truculence had returned.

"Well, Blest," he said, "I think we're going to get it over before morning, after all."

He did not actually say, "and we could have dispensed with

your services, my dear sir," but his manner implied the words as surely as if they had been spoken.

David hardly noticed the rather childish hint. His mind was racing on to the morning headlines, to the trial, to Judy's horror-stricken, terrified face, and he felt cold and helpless.

Bloomer, on the other hand, was in a particularly sensitive mood.

"Wait a minute, Inspector," he said, in a tone which no sergeant of any police force in the world should ever employ when addressing a superior officer. "Before you go any further I think you ought to listen to me. I've got a very important piece of infor-mation. I've been turning over my old notebooks, and I've found something that's going to revolutionize this case."

Inspector Winn turned round slowly and surveyed the ex-policeman.

A braver but more intelligent man than Bloomer would have quailed before that glance. But Bloomer was elated quite as much as his superior and hurried on blissfully while David waited for the blow to fall.

"Oh, I've found something of great interest," said the ex-sergeant. "Something that's going to make you sit up."

"Bloomer!" Winn's voice was terrible. "You're drunk. Get out of here before I throw you out."

The ex-sergeant stopped in full flight. His mouth fell slowly open, his small eyes puckered at first, to open wide afterwards in blank incredulity.

David held his peace. He saw no point in interfering at this juncture. The sight of the old man goggling before him seemed to move Winn to further rage.

"Get out!" he said, his voice shaking, and it occurred to David that this fury was largely due to the fact that Bloomer had presumed to address him as an equal in front of a Scotland Yard man.

Had the ex-sergeant been strictly sober it is possible that he might have drawn back with sufficient grace at this point to mollify the local man, and all would still have been well.

But Bloomer was far from sober, and he was also very pleased with himself. His eyes narrowed again after their first surprise, and a grim and particularly unpleasant expression settled over his stolid features.

"*All—right*, sir," he said, throwing in the courtesy form of address as an afterthought. "All—right, Inspector. Good-night to you."

He shuffled out of the room, his enormous carpet slippers flapping over the parquetry.

Inspector Winn glanced sharply at David, but no glimmer of a smile showed on that young man's expressionless face. He cleared his throat noisily.

"These house detectives are impossible at the best of times," he said. "That man is a disgrace to the hotel. I shall report him to the manager. But the first thing to do is to get our man. Everything's ready. I've got a couple of men outside. Shall we go up at once?"

David hesitated, but he did not speak, and the other man, noticing his diffidence, hastened to justify himself.

"I don't think there's any question of there not being sufficient evidence," he said stiffly. "After all, there's the girl's testimony, and the gun was found directly beneath his window. We should be doing less than our duty if we didn't pull him in at once."

"Oh, quite," said David. "Quite."

His mind was very far away. For the first time in his life personal considerations kept forcing themselves into matters of duty, and he felt bewildered and at sea.

"I think we'll question him here and then take him along to the station afterwards," Winn continued, and, without waiting for David's acquiescence, turned towards the door.

Before he could reach it, however, it had been thrown open, and a person who, David guessed, must be the manager of the Empress shot into the room as though he had been precipitated from a catapult. He must have been an odd-looking individual at the best of times, but at the present moment, with his short black hair standing on end and his sallow face tinged with a greenish shade, he made an unforgettable picture.

He was a fat man, faultlessly clothed in a dinner-jacket suit. He was quivering with apprehension and almost incapable of speech as he waved his plump hands at the two detectives rather as though he were attempting to mesmerize them.

"I've just heard," he exploded at last. "I have just heard, and I cannot have an arrest in my hotel. It is monstrous—unheard of! Terrible!—and I won't have it. I won't have it here. I can't help it. I won't argue with you," he continued, although neither of the inspectors had said a word to him. "This is my hotel. My dear sirs, consider what it will mean to me if there is an arrest. The whole place will be empty by this time tomorrow."

He paused for a moment, and when they said nothing, sank down in a chair and passed an immense white handkerchief over his face.

"It's no use arguing. I won't consider it," he said. "You can talk as much as you like. What I say I mean. No arrest is possible in this hotel."

Inspector Winn coughed. The manager of the Empress had the ear of the chief constable. Therefore it was as well to move tactfully.

He was still embarrassed by David's presence, too. The young man's stolid indifference to the little scenes he had just witnessed got on Inspector Winn's nerves, and he had no means of finding out whether this representative of Scotland Yard was amused, bored, or silently criticizing.

"Arrest, Mr. Populof?" he said mildly. "Aren't you making a mistake? We're only anxious to get this thing over. You know that. And you have a guest here, a Mr. Lionel Birch, whom we're very anxious to interrogate. I think we'll go upstairs and see him, if you don't mind. Don't be alarmed. There won't be any noise. If by chance we do have to ask him to accompany us, you can rely on our discretion. None of your other guests need ever know anything has taken place."

The manager mopped his forehead, sighed, groaned, and exhibited every sign of giving way completely to his emotions.

"If I could only rely on that," he said.

"But of course you can." Inspector Winn was in his element. "We'll go straight upstairs now, very quietly. No one need ever know anything about it. We shan't be a moment. But it's very important that we should have a word with Mr. Birch at once. After all, Mr. Populof, we want this thing cleared up at once, don't we?"

"Good heavens, yes. The sooner the better. You gentlemen don't understand. This means ruin for me—ruin. What will my regular patrons say of me if I have a murderer in my hotel? Still, Inspector, you understand there must be no arrest? If you want to lock the man up, you must take him away and do it somewhere else."

The complete illogicality of this announcement did not seem to occur to any of the three men, or, at any rate, nobody smiled. David was much too absorbed in his own thoughts to pay much attention to the hysterical manager, Inspector Winn was not blessed with much sense of humour, while Mr. Populof evidently had none at all.

Inspector Winn turned to David.

"I think we'll go up, Blest," he said. "Shall we?"

"I will come with you," Mr. Populof insisted.

Winn put his foot down. "I think not, sir," he said. "This is a confidential police matter. Perhaps you'll wait for us down here?"

After a certain amount of persuasion Mr. Populof consented to remain downstairs and for the third time that evening David walked up the broad staircase of the Empress Hotel and climbed to the second floor.

As they reached the second floor and walked down the broad

corridor, two plainclothes men following them at a discreet distance, the full force of the terrible situation in which he found himself burst into David's consciousness. He loved Judy: the fact stood out clearly in his mind. His future happiness was bound up in her. And yet here he was walking down a hotel corridor at four o'clock to arrest her father on a charge of murder.

There were beads of sweat upon his forehead when he paused outside room number fifty. With a smile of grim satisfaction upon his face Inspector Winn raised his fist and tapped upon the door.

The four men waited. They knew there was no other exit from the room save the window, and from that there was a thirty-foot drop into the police-lined street below.

There was no reply to the first tap, and the inspector knocked again, more loudly this time. David felt his own heart beating ridiculously loudly. It was a nerve-racking situation.

Still there was no reply. Inspector Winn frowned.

"We can't make a noise. Better go in."

He drew a pass key from his pocket and fitted it into the lock.

"Carefully," he whispered. "He may have a second gun."

The door opened softly, and Winn and David, followed by the plainclothes men, stepped swiftly inside. The room was in darkness, and as David stretched out his hand and switched on the light a startled exclamation escaped the local man.

David stared round him in bewilderment. The room presented an extraordinary scene. Not only was it deserted—so much was evident at a first glance—but it was completely ransacked. Bedclothes strewed the floor. Every drawer lay out upon its side. The wardrobe door hung crazily open. The mattress had been displaced, revealing the wire springs beneath. The windows were wide open, and the curtains swung lazily in the draught.

But of Lionel Birch or any of his belongings there was no trace whatever.

Inspector Winn turned to David. His face was very pale, and

his small eyes were darker than usual with mingled disappointment and bewilderment.

"What happened?" he said. "He made a quick getaway,
didn't he?"

David said nothing. His blue eyes were characteristically lazy-
looking, and the thought which ran obstinately through his mind,
and which had worried him since he had first set eyes upon the
scene, was that when one packs in a great hurry one hardly wastes
a great deal of precious time in completely dismantling one's bed
and hurling the blankets and linen into every conceivable corner
of the room.

The more he thought about it the more convinced he was that
there was something quite incomprehensible and extraordinary
about Judy Wellington's father's flight from justice.

Inspector Winn cut into his thoughts.

"Lost him," he said, his voice unsteady and uncontrollable with
fury. "Slipped through our very fingers. But we'll get him. We'll
get him if we have to comb the whole of England. This proves he's
our man, anyway, and I'll pull him in. I'll pull him in if it's the last
thing I do."

8

THE TERRACE SUN TRAP

"MY DEAR CHILD, you don't look at all well this morning. Come and sit by me and watch the sea. It's perfectly beautiful here: sunny and yet cool."

Marguerite Ferney, in a white cotton gown, miraculously cut, and trimmed with a scarlet and white spotted kerchief enhancing the dazzling fairness of her skin and hair, came running down a little flight of stone steps built into the rock itself and hurried to meet Judy as she walked along the lower promenade.

Judy looked pale and wan. It was far too hot, even for an invalid, to stick to the eternal squirrel coat, and she had replaced it with a thick white one over her cotton frock.

Judy had been forced out for a little walk. The atmosphere of the hotel was stifling in spite of every modern device to keep it cool. But out here it seemed almost worse.

Marguerite Ferney went on talking, and her cool loveliness was curiously attractive.

"Look," she said. "Doesn't that fascinate you? It's the most comfortable place in the world to sit."

Judy smiled at her shyly, and, glancing over her shoulder,

looked up at the little oasis in the sunlight which the other woman indicated.

This was a tiny grass-covered ledge, a natural beauty which the gardeners of the hotel had been quick to enhance. It was situated some twenty feet below the main terrace and was really nothing more than a little pocket in the cliff, halfway between the hotel terrace and the second promenade.

A collection of rock plants had been persuaded to grow all round it, and there was a little plot of grass in the middle which was occupied at the moment by two extremely comfortable-looking deck chairs, a pile of magazines, and an immense gaily-coloured umbrella which cast a comfortable shadow in the midst of the blazing sunlight.

It certainly did look extraordinarily inviting. Judy hesitated and was lost. Marguerite Ferney was a person who was used to getting her own way.

"Come along," she said. "Come along and sit down."

Judy found herself coaxed up into the little oasis beneath the wall of the hotel garden.

"I found this place yesterday," Miss Ferney remarked, helping her into a chair, "and as soon as I saw it I said to myself, 'That's the place for me to sit.' So I interviewed the manager and had it all fixed up. Very sensible of me, don't you think?"

Judy regarded this brilliant creature with a certain amount of awe. She had been a little put off at their first meeting on the evening before, but Marguerite Ferney's personality was of the effervescent and dangerous type which inspires confidence very easily. Judy found her extraordinarily easy to talk to and began to like her very much.

"Yes, it's beautiful," she said, settling down in the depths of her cushioned chair and looking out over the sparkling water where a fleet of tiny fishing boats gleamed like white butterflies in the sun. "It was awfully nice of you to ask me to come up here, Miss Ferney."

"My dear child, of course not. I was dying for somebody to talk to, and you looked nearly as lonely as I was. Tell me, what's happened to your handsome young cousin? You did tell me he was a cousin, didn't you? The one I met last night."

In spite of herself Judy flushed.

"No, he's no relation," she said.

"Oh dear." Miss Ferney looked contrite. "I do hope I didn't disturb a flirtation. But he's extraordinarily handsome, my dear. I quite lost my heart to him."

Judy's discomfort increased. She had been trying not to think too much of David and had found it extremely difficult. And, try as she would, she could not stifle the little pain at her heart whenever she thought of him.

Marguerite Ferney rattled on.

"Tell me, my dear," she said, "what are you doing all alone down here? You are quite alone, aren't you? I mean except for the extremely handsome young man."

Judy hesitated. She was usually the most discreet of mortals, but, although Marguerite Ferney irritated her intensely when she spoke of David, she did seem extraordinarily guileless, and it certainly had been kind of her to ask her up to this delightful little private terrace.

"Oh no," she said. "My guardian's staying here, Sir Leo Thyn."

"Oh, really? You're staying for your health, I suppose?" The other woman's eyes were fixed on Judy's face, and the girl felt that she had penetrated her secret. She reddened under her make-up.

"Yes," she said deliberately. "I've never been very well."

"A permanent invalid? Oh, my dear child, how tragic! You must promise to come and sit up here whenever you feel like it. I shall be delighted to have you, really I shall. And now tell me all about yourself."

Judy began to wish more and more that she had never accepted Miss Ferney's invitation in the first place, yet in spite of herself she could not help being attracted to the other woman. She watched her thoughtfully under half-closed lids.

Marguerite Ferney seemed completely unaware of her scrutiny, and the expression upon her face was guileless and friendly. When she went on to speak it was about trivial matters, and Judy reproached herself for being unduly suspicious.

Marguerite Ferney was an adept at making people talk, and she practised her wiles on Judy with a skill which made the girl's ingenuous attempts at reticence seem absurd.

When her fears and suspicions were completely allayed and she was thinking of nothing save the charm of her new friend, Miss Ferney played her trump card.

"Quite a lot of excitement in the town last night," she said. "I do hope it won't be bad for all these poor people who are trying to make a living out of the holiday visitors. And yet one never knows. People are so morbid, it may even draw crowds to the place. One never can tell. You've read about it, of course?"

She turned over the pages of a newspaper which lay upon her knee and presently handed it to the girl. The first thing Judy saw staring up at her from the page was a police photograph of the man whom she imagined she was going to marry, and underneath, in bold type:

"Johnny Deane, alias 'The Major,' was found shot in a small West-bourne hotel at a late hour last night."

The paper, an early copy of the *Evening Telegram,* slipped through her fingers, and Marguerite Ferney, who had been watching her carefully, bent forward.

"My dear child," she said, "what is it? Did you know him? Oh, you poor little thing, you must tell me all about it. I insist. Perhaps there's something I can do to help."

Judy picked up the paper again and forced herself to read the headline. Then a strangled cry escaped her as another announcement caught her eye.

"The police are particularly anxious to interview a man called Lionel

Birch, who was staying at the Empress Hotel at the time of the crime. He left soon afterwards, but so far his whereabouts has not been ascertained."

"Miss Wellington, you're as white as a sheet. You look as though you're going to faint. Tell me all about this. I have a lot of influence in all sorts of directions. Perhaps I can help you. Won't you confide in me, my dear?"

The words died upon her lips. A shadow had fallen across her lap, and, looking up, she became aware of a tall, thin old man in a grey alpaca suit, who stood at the top of the steps, his eyes bent searchingly upon her.

Saxon Marsh was not an attractive-looking person at the best of times, and to look up suddenly and find him peering at one might well have made any ordinary woman quail; but Marguerite Ferney was far from being ordinary.

"Yes?" she said inquiringly in her softest tones.

Saxon Marsh continued to stare at her for some moments before he spoke. Then he said unexpectedly:

"Which of you two is Miss Judy Wellington?"

Judy sat up stiffly, and he turned his head and looked at her.

"Ah," he said. "Miss Wellington, your guardian is looking everywhere for you, my dear. I think you'd better go to him. I daresay you'll find him in his rooms."

Judy started to her feet. Even the glorious weather seemed part of the terrible nightmare into which she had been plunged by the terrible paragraph in the newspaper. She barely looked at Saxon Marsh, but with a muttered and incoherent apology to Miss Ferney she turned and fled.

Saxon Marsh remained where he was. For some time he stood quite still, looking down at the woman without speaking.

Marguerite Ferney showed no signs of irritation or alarm but returned his stare steadily.

After a while he stepped forward uninvited and seated himself in the chair which Judy had vacated, stretching out his long, skeleton-like legs and folding his thin yellow hands across his body.

"A charming little girl, is she not?" he remarked at last. "So anxious to talk about herself. So charming and engaging in all her ways."

Marguerite Ferney did not answer. She had taken a tiny silver vanity case from her bag and was peering thoughtfully at her flawless complexion in the tiny glass it contained.

"You don't know me," Saxon Marsh went on in the same even, precise tone in which he might have commented on the weather. "I really don't think that matters. But I have a proposition to put up to you, Miss Ferney: one which, if you are as wise as I have reason to believe, you will accept with enthusiasm."

Still the woman did not speak or even glance in his direction. She seemed to be engrossed in the slender line of her left eyebrow.

"First of all, perhaps you will forgive me if I come straight to a rather delicate matter," the man continued placidly. "Your finances, Miss Ferney, are in a very—shall we say unsatisfactory condition?"

The woman nodded coolly.

"That is true," she said.

"Ah." The man pounced upon the admission. "In that case, Miss Ferney, you will, I am sure, be particularly interested in what I am going to say now. I have a very difficult and delicate mission to entrust to the right person. Once it is brought to a satisfactory conclusion there will be a great deal of money in it, both for me and my messenger. It requires tact, and that is why I feel that a woman, a clever, unscrupulous woman, is the person I need. It would necessitate this lady going to Australia within the next fortnight. The matter is urgent, you see. In all the trip would take the best part of a year, but the reward would be magnificent. Now, Miss Ferney, what do you say? Shall I continue?"

Marguerite Ferney shut the little silver case in her hand with a snap and put it back in her handbag. Then she leant back in her chair and turned her head slowly until her eyes rested squarely upon the man's face.

"I must understand this thing completely," she said in a voice that was dangerously calm. "First of all, you want me to leave the country: that is to say, to go to Australia and to remain away for the best part of a year. During that time I am to undertake some delicate but not, I suppose, dangerous, mission."

There was the merest hint of sarcasm in her tone on the last phrase.

Saxon Marsh nodded.

"Exactly," he said. "And the remuneration would be enormous; quite enough to get you out of your present difficulties and establish you permanently in the manner to which—er—you have become accustomed."

Marguerite Ferney lay back in her chair and laughed. She laughed with genuine amusement, her pale face flushing, and her big, rather hard eyes suffusing with tears of mirth.

Saxon Marsh looked at her closely, striving to detect a false note of hysteria in the sound, but found none. Miss Ferney was genuinely amused.

"Dear Mr. Saxon Marsh!" she said at last. "Do you too believe that all women are necessarily fools?"

The use of his name when he clearly thought himself to be unrecognized startled the man, and he frowned.

Miss Ferney continued.

"No, I'm sorry," she said. "I'm afraid I can't undertake your 'delicate, tactful mission' which was to make us both so rich. You see, my dear Mr. Marsh, I happen to be very busy. I have a little matter of my own on hand which requires a certain amount of tact in itself, and it too, I hope, will not prove unremunerative."

After the first frown of annoyance Saxon Marsh did not show any other sign of emotion. He continued to look at the girl but with a curious, detached interest, as though he hardly considered her a real person.

"I'm sorry you can't entertain my proposition," he said. "You seemed such an intelligent girl. Don't you think it would be an idea, Miss Ferney, to work with me instead of against me?"

The girl sat forward in her chair and turned her head so that her eyes met his, and people on the beach below might well have thought that they were two old friends, or perhaps father and daughter, chatting amicably about the most trivial of subjects.

"There is only so much money," she said. "Do you understand?"

Saxon Marsh rose to his feet.

"Miss Ferney," he said in his silkiest tones, "may I advise you that it would be wisest for you, best for your health, shall we say, if you left Westbourne, or at any rate kept out of the way of Miss Judy Wellington?"

Saxon Marsh had unpleasant eyes, and even Miss Ferney, who was not afraid of anything on earth, experienced a faint thrill of distaste and apprehension as she looked into them.

"Mr. Marsh," she said, "you amuse me. I have often noticed that when men become very wealthy they are apt to lose all sense of proportion. I would like to remind you that this is respectable Westbourne, in safe, respectable England, and it is the twentieth century. Melodrama, don't you think, is rather out of place?"

Saxon Marsh raised his head and looked up at the blue sky above the terrace. The ornamental wall of the hotel garden was silhouetted against that vivid blue twenty feet above his head. It was a very fine wall, of grey stone overhung with creeping rock plants and punctuated every now and again with huge stone urns also filled with flowers.

Directly above him, or rather directly above the chair in which Miss Ferney sat, was one of these huge urns, kept in position upon the wall by its own weight and the growth of lichen and moss which surrounded its base.

As Saxon Marsh looked at it now, filled with scarlet geraniums gleaming so bravely against the vivid sky, his pale eyes flickered.

And then, after a pause during which he turned and gazed thoughtfully out to sea, he shrugged his shoulders.

"Miss Ferney," he said, "you're a clever woman. Just how clever I don't know. But I have a feeling I may soon find out. Perhaps you will think over my suggestion. After all, remember the old proverb, 'A bird in the hand is worth two in chancery.' Perhaps I may come and talk to you again some time," he added. "This is a charming spot. Tell me, do you often sit here?"

Marguerite Ferney, who had not followed his glance and who knew nothing of the old-fashioned ornamental wall above her head, and had probably never noticed the heavy stone urn with its load of blood-red geraniums, answered frankly enough.

"Why, yes," she said. "I always sit here. It's my special corner."

Saxon Marsh's smile broadened.

"Usually alone?" he inquired.

"Usually alone," said Marguerite Ferney innocently.

9

THE PRIVATE INVESTIGATOR

INSPECTOR BLEST, hot, dusty, and badly in need of sleep, strode into the lounge of the Arcadian about three o'clock that afternoon and, avoiding Old Charlie and the manager, who were both moved by a desire to gossip with him, hurried up the stair-case. The lift he disdained, not because he particularly wanted to walk, but because even the lift boy's eyes had contained a gleam of curiosity as they rested upon him, and he was not in the mood to repulse with politeness.

David was worried. He had made up his mind to speak to Judy. She would have to know the situation, have to realize that sooner or later she would be cross-questioned by the police and that sooner or later the secret of her birth must be revealed.

David wanted to spare her at least the shock. Thinking it over, he realized that he would not be able to trust himself to listen while Inspector Winn ploughed tactlessly over the girl's feelings. It was an unpleasant task David had set himself, and he was not looking forward to it, but he pressed on.

He had had a nerve-racking day. Inspector Winn's oath, "comb England if necessary for Lionel Birch," looked as though it would give the Westbourne police many weary months of work if it was to be fulfilled.

Lionel Birch had disappeared completely and utterly, leaving no trace save the disordered room. Winn and his minions had scoured the place, interviewing everyone who might possibly be of use to them. But their task was incredibly difficult. It was not easy to obtain descriptions of everyone leaving a busy seaside town in the height of the season. Dozens of excursion trains, scores of charabancs had sped out of Westbourne the night before. And to make matters even more difficult, half the town seemed to have been in fancy dress. Even the booking clerk at the Empress could not say for certain which of his clients had come in before the crime had been discovered or who had gone out. His mind was a maze of Harlequins, Red Indian chiefs, Queen Elizabeths, and Mickey Mice.

When David reached the landing he sought and turned down the corridor towards Judy's room, he had dismissed all these things from his mind. He was thinking only of Judy and wondering how to tell her the terrible truth which had to be told, wondering how he could hurt her least.

He was within sight of her door when it opened, and his heart leapt, as it always did, at the prospect of seeing her. But the next moment anticipation was turned to bewilderment and a growing sense of complete stupefaction for there emerged out of Judy's door two completely unexpected persons.

One was a jovial old rascal in a fisherman's jersey and slacks, a peaked cap on the back of his head, and a broad smile on his bewhiskered face; and the other was no less a person than ex-Sergeant Bloomer himself, very solemn and portentous in his best clothes and carrying as carefully as though it had been a bomb nothing more nor less than the plainclothes policeman's proverbial bowler hat.

David paused in his stride. The element of the completely unexpected which seemed to have become quite a feature of the case was once more manifest. How on earth had Bloomer got on to Judy, and what in the name of good fortune could he possibly have had to say to her?

He had no time for conjecture, however, for the odd pair had by this time come abreast of him, and Bloomer's little round eyes had widened considerably as he recognized the Scotland Yard man.

But if David's appearance was a shock to him he preserved his composure remarkably well.

"Afternoon, sir," he said blandly, pausing, and a smile spreading over his plump red face. "You're staying 'ere, aren't you, sir? It's a very fine hotel. Makes us look right shabby."

His companion had paused also, and in the cool shadow of the corridor his unkempt appearance looked very out of place.

Bloomer made no attempt to introduce him but seemed to see nothing odd about his presence.

David was more mystified than ever.

"What are you doing here, Bloomer?" he inquired. "Have you given up your job at the Empress in favor of the Arcadian?"

"Me? Oh no, sir. I'm on leave. Me afternoon out, the management calls it. No sense of dignity, these commercial people, 'ave they?"

He would have moved on, but David was in the way, and the young man did not attempt to move. Bloomer became confidential.

"As a matter of fact, sir," he murmured, lowering his voice to the husky rumble to which David had become accustomed, "I'm pursuing a little line of investigation of me own. Just because my cooperation was flouted the other night it doesn't mean that I've lorst interest. Oh well, I said to meself, if you're not wanted, Bloomer, 'e can manage without you, but that doesn't mean you're going to stand by and see mistakes made all along the line, does it? Oh dear me no! So here I am on the job, sir, and I hope you won't mention it."

David quite appreciated Bloomer's position. He no longer belonged to the regular force, it was true, and really, strictly speaking, he owed no loyalty to anyone but the hotel manager who employed him; but his cheerful assumption that David owed nothing to Inspector Winn either shocked the young inspector's rigid sense of police etiquette.

"Really, Bloomer, this is outrageous," he said. "I think you certainly ought to go to Inspector Winn and tell him all you know, and prefix it with a handsome apology for your manner last night."

The words cost David a certain amount of effort and were prompted only by a sense of loyalty, for it was certainly not to his own personal interest that Bloomer should go to Winn with a piece of information that would take that irascible officer straight to Judy herself.

Bloomer hesitated. Then a broad if somewhat shamefaced grin spread over his features.

"I certainly ought to apologize," he said at last. "I made a reg'lar fool of meself one way and another. But I don't think I'll go back to Inspector Winn if you don't mind, Captain. In the first place, you see, I made a mistake. It was really lucky he didn't hear me out, as it happens."

David stared at him. "You made a mistake?" he said.

"Yes," said ex-Sergeant Bloomer blandly. "It was me memory again. I thought of it afterwards. That fellow the inspector's hunting for wasn't the man I thought 'e was. Shows you how careful you've got to be, doesn't it, sir?"

David frowned. The man was lying: so much was obvious. But why should he? What possible motive could he have for suddenly withdrawing his evidence which had come out so spontaneously at the time? David glanced at the bowler hat and thought he could guess the explanation. Ex-Sergeant Bloomer was fancying himself as a full-blown detective, and, having taken offence at Inspector

Winn, had decided to handle the case and make a bid for glory on his own account.

David thought it his duty to remonstrate.

"You'll never do any good trying to work without the police, Bloomer," he said. "You'll only get into trouble. I should cut it out if I were you."

"Work without the police, sir?" Bloomer looked shocked, but it was the same degree of polite astonishment which habitual criminals sometimes employ when speaking to a police officer whom they consider overinquisitive, but whom at the same time they do not wish to offend.

David recognized that tone and recognized Bloomer's frame of mind.

"I see you're obstinate," he said.

Ex-Sergeant Bloomer looked hurt.

"Obstinate? *Me*, Captain? Oh dear me no. I'm only trying to 'elp. Come along, George. Good-afternoon, sir."

The person addressed as George grinned foolishly and shambled off with Bloomer.

David was nettled, but in spite of his irritation he could not help feeling that there was something likable about old Bloomer. He was a wholehearted old rascal, at any rate, and Winn had certainly treated him in a very cavalier fashion.

He had just turned back to his original project and was advancing upon Judy's door when the second impediment to his interview with her that afternoon came hurtling down the corridor behind him.

The man moved so rapidly and brushed past David so sharply that their shoulders touched. The next instant he had forestalled the inspector and was tapping loudly on Judy's door.

David recognized him instantly. It was Sir Leo Thyn. Although he had only a fleeting glimpse of him—for the girl's door was opened almost immediately, and the baronet stepped inside and slammed the door behind him with unnecessary violence—David had time to observe the extraordinary change which had taken place in the old man since he had last seen him.

Sir Leo was positively haggard. The vivid colour had vanished from his face, leaving it veined but pallid, and his extraordinarily precipitate rush upon the door suggested extreme nervous tension. David raised his eyebrows, and for the second time that day the conviction came back to him that Sir Leo knew a great deal more about the whole inexplicable business than anyone seemed to imagine.

David was irritated. It was evident that he could not speak to Judy just now, but it was also very clear that such an interview was vitally necessary. He stepped into his own room and stood thinking. He would wait, he decided, until Sir Leo had gone, and then tackle the girl.

He walked over to the open window and stood looking down into the garden with the sea beyond. But his mind was very far away from the glittering panorama spread out before him. Sir Leo, he felt sure, had not recognized him. The corridor was dark, and the man had clearly been in such a state of nerves that his mind was only fixed upon his immediate objective.

From where he stood scraps of conversation floated in to him through the open window of the other room. David listened openly, his scruples completely set aside because of the tremendous importance of the situation. Even so, it was impossible to hear much.

Judy was inaudible. He could hear her voice, but it was pitched so low that he could catch no separate word.

Sir Leo, on the other hand, while using a rumbling monotone most of the time, occasionally raised his voice, and disjointed phrases, shrill with hysteria, reached the inspector quite clearly.

"It's imperative," David heard him say again and again. "Imperative. I insist. I tell you I order it."

There was a murmur of protest from Judy, and then a few

words from Sir Leo, sounding as clear as though they had been spoken in his ear.

"You must not speak to her. She is dangerous."

It was not the words themselves, although they were odd in the circumstances, which caught David's attention. It was the tone in which they were uttered, a tone of fear.

David had heard men who had been frightened before, and could hardly have been mistaken. The high, thin note of alarm sounded as shrill as though it had been played upon a trumpet, and he wondered who it was who filled Sir Leo with such tremendous apprehension.

David moved closer to the window in the hope of hearing more, but in this he was frustrated, for the voices became more and more indistinct, and it sounded as though the two had moved farther back into the room.

David stared idly at the gardens below. The sun streamed into the room, and he noticed that the sunblinds were down over practically all the other windows below him. He could see their striped canvas lengths foreshortened as he peered down upon them. The whole hotel seemed to be taking a siesta. The gardens were deserted, and far below, at the foot of the cliffs, he knew that the beach was covered with lazy, supine figures bathing in the afternoon sun.

A heat haze hung over the entire scene.

He was still watching the garden idly, his mind on the drone of tantalizing conversation in the next room. He had seriously thought of moving back the huge wardrobe and listening blatantly at the inner door through which he had once burst so unceremoniously upon the girl. But as this necessitated his making a certain amount of noise he decided that it was a risk he could not take, since it was manifestly important that Sir Leo should not be put *on* his guard.

He returned again to the window and noticed for the first time that the terrace garden was not deserted. The tall, thin figure of a man in an old-fashioned grey alpaca suit was strolling languidly across the lawn.

David had never accounted himself the possessor of any psychic gift, but the fact remained that, although he had never seen Saxon Marsh before, and now only had a very foreshortened view of him, from the first moment the young inspector set eyes upon that curious stooping figure he became interested in the man.

It was not that he did anything at all suspicious. On the contrary, he walked slowly and apparently without purpose. Yet it was odd how sinister that solitary grey-clad figure managed to appear as he walked slowly over the grass.

He reached the wall, and, as David watched him, his mind still more than half upon the muttered conversation in the next room, stared out to sea.

Some few feet farther along the wall was a huge stone urn filled with scarlet geraniums. There were six urns in all set along the low wall in front of the hotel, but each contained a different variety of flower, and David especially noticed the vivid scarlet flowers standing out clearly against the glittering background of sea far beyond.

As the young detective watched the solitary figure of the tall, elderly man he noticed for the first time that the other did not seem to be well. Although he was much too far away to see the other's face, he noticed that he reeled and put his hand up to his head as though oppressed by the heat.

Presently he seemed to straighten himself with an effort and to walk on along the narrow path by the side of the wall. His movement was erratic, however, and when at last he came up level with the urn of geraniums he stood reeling. He put out his hand to steady himself and then collapsed, the full force of his weight hitting the top of the urn.

A smothered exclamation escaped the young inspector. It seemed that the man must topple over the low wall onto the promenade some twenty feet below. But this was not to be. With a tremendous effort, quite extraordinary, David thought vaguely, for a man so overcome, he righted himself, but not before the urn itself had clattered over the edge of the wall.

There was a dull crash, and David thought he heard a muffled scream, but thought nothing of it at the time, for at this point his mind was jerked back from the scene outside the window to matters which directly concerned him.

From the room next door he heard a muffled exclamation from the girl; then a sharp angry phrase, the sense of which he could not catch, from Sir Leo; and afterwards, while his senses were keyed up and he stood straining his ears, complete silence for a full minute.

Then there was a crash as the girl's door slammed violently and the automatic lock shot home.

On noiseless feet David crossed his room and opened his own door the fraction of an inch. He heard thick heavy footsteps hurrying away down the corridor and, opening the door a little wider, made out the stocky figure of Sir Leo hurrying to the lift.

David waited until the coast was clear and then slipped out into the deserted corridor and tapped gently on Judy's door.

There was no reply, and he tapped again, a little more loudly this time.

Still there was no answer from within, and a sense of bewilderment not untinged with alarm passed over him. With his own ears he had heard Judy talking to Sir Leo, and with his own eyes he had seen the baronet departing alone.

He knocked again, fiercely this time.

There was no movement inside the room, but, listening intently, he thought he heard a faint muffled cry from somewhere within.

David felt suddenly cold.

"Judy!" he called. "Judy!"

This time there was no sound. Panic seized David. The door

was heavy and not easy to break in, even had such a course been in any way desirable in the circumstances.

He slipped back into his own room, pulled back the wardrobe and tried the inner door. It was locked. Outside the window there was a considerable amount of commotion, but David was far too absorbed in his own problem to notice it. He examined the catch feverishly, and to his delight saw that it was one of those thumb-spring affairs and of no great strength. He put his shoulder to it and pushed, realizing instinctively that silence was important.

He burst into the other room at last and stared about him. At first glance he thought it was empty. The big, airy room was tidy and bare.

"Judy," he said hoarsely.

And then his eye fell upon the door of a cupboard built into the wall by the fireplace. In a moment he had reached it and had swept back the bolt.

Judy was inside, Judy with her hands tied behind her and a handkerchief thrust into her mouth.

He pulled her out into the room and released her. His face was grim, and there was a dangerous expression in his lazy blue eyes. The girl took a deep breath.

"Oh, David," she said. "Oh, my dear, what a blessing you came!"

The young man stood looking down at her. The extraordinary discovery had shaken him more than he realized. She looked so extraordinarily frail and helpless standing there, her honey-coloured curls dishevelled, her face flushed, and her eyes unusu-ally bright.

He put his hands on her shoulders.

"Now," he said, "what's the explanation of this? No more beating about the bush, Judy. You've got to tell me. Good heavens, if you'd been left in there for any length of time you'd have suffo-cated. I want the whole truth and nothing but the truth."

The girl avoided his eyes. Instead of looking at him she glanced fearfully at the door behind him.

"Quick, David, there's no time to lose," she said. "I can't tell you anything now, my dear. There's not time. We've got to get right out of here before he comes back. He only put me in there so that I shouldn't get out and escape. He'll be back any moment."

In spite of himself David was impressed by the urgency in her tone. However, he stuck to his point.

"It's no good, Judy," he said. "This is the last straw. I've got a lot to tell you, but first of all there's a great deal that you must tell me. Things are bad, Judy, but I'm going to see you through if you'll only let me."

He had given himself away completely, and now, as he saw the expression in her eyes, he realized the futility of pretending to himself or to her any longer.

"You know I love you," he said gravely.

He saw the colour come and vanish in her face. Then her eyes met his, very steady and sincere.

"Yes," she said. "I know, and I'm glad. I'm afraid I love you too, David. But it's no good. I've got to get out of here at once, before Sir Leo comes back. One day you shall know everything, I promise you, but not now. Oh, please trust me. Help me to get out of here at once."

Inspector David Blest was not easily put off his purpose as a rule, but, to do him justice, the circumstances were definitely unusual.

The girl was clearly panic-stricken, and after that brief exciting moment when she had admitted her love for him the bewildered David was prepared to do anything in the world for her.

He stepped back across the room, closed the communicating door, and placed a chair across it so that the broken lock might not be immediately obvious to a newcomer.

Meanwhile Judy had combed her hair and snatched up a coat. She rebolted the cupboard door, and then together they slipped out into the corridor.

Judy was almost running, and he was forced to hurry to keep up with her.

"What are you going to do?" he demanded urgently. "I must know, Judy. I insist."

She turned to him pleadingly, her eyes meeting his.

"Trust me," she whispered. "Oh please, please, trust me."

And then, before he could stop her, she had turned and fled, not down the staircase as might have been supposed, but up towards the third floor.

David started after her, but she waved him back, and he saw her face suddenly grey with fear.

"He's coming," she said. "He's coming. Don't let him catch me, David, please!"

He would have followed her, but at that moment there was a considerable commotion on the floor below, and the sound of excited voices reached him.

The young Scotland Yard man peered over the banisters and looked down upon an excited group of people carrying something carefully up the staircase. From where he stood he had a clear view of the scene. Two sturdy hotel officials, one of them the burly commissionaire, were carrying the swooning figure of a woman. Behind them hovered a man who was obviously a doctor, and surrounding the whole quartet was a crowd of guests, hotel servants, and people who had obviously come in from the promenade.

As the procession rounded the bend, the woman's face came into David's line of vision, and he saw to his surprise that it was none other than the beautiful Marguerite Ferney.

David hurried down to meet the crowd, his curiosity thoroughly aroused. The onlookers were only too anxious to tell him what happened.

"Just missed her," said one little man. "Might have killed her. Smashed her to a pulp. I expect it was the umbrella that broke the fall. It's shock, really. That's why we didn't bring her up by the lift."

David was still puzzled, and his informant opened his little round eyes in astonishment.

"Why, don't you know anything about it?" he inquired. "Oh, a nasty accident! Might have killed her."

They were standing in a corner of the staircase, and the crowd was still pressing past them. The little man was in a quandary, torn between the desire to tell the story and not to lose his place near the casualty.

"It was the flower pot," he explained. "Great big stone flower pot fell off the hotel wall just by where she was sitting. It smashed one deck chair to atoms. It's a miracle to me how it happened. There's going to be a lot of inquiry about this, I can tell you. Not a breath of wind—nothing. Rank carelessness, that's what it amounts to. Excuse me, I must get on."

With the awful inquisitiveness of his breed he scrambled on up the staircase after the departed procession, and the last David saw of him he was worming his way through the crowd, his straw hat still on the back of his head, back to his old advantageous position.

David walked slowly and thoughtfully downstairs. The scene he had watched in the hotel garden came back vividly to his mind. He saw again the tall thin figure in the grey alpaca suit and remembered afresh that extraordinary recovery when the man, so obviously overcome by faintness, had yet saved himself from going over the wall with the stone urn. Was it quite the accident it had seemed?

The fact which leapt to his mind and particularly aroused his interest was the all-important one that it was Marguerite Ferney who had been so nearly killed. Marguerite Ferney was in some inexplicable way connected with the mystery that surrounded Sir Leo and Judy, and in that case, if the accident had been no accident but a deliberate attempt at murder, then the man in the grey alpaca suit was in some way connected with the business also and merited David's attention.

He strolled out onto the terrace, the whole hotel behind him still buzzing with excitement over the accident. Things were happening so rapidly, clues being strewn so liberally in his path, that he hardly knew how to sort them out. He was debarred from serious consideration just then, however, by the sight of a little group standing at the far end of the terrace by the empty space on the wall where the stone urn of geraniums had once stood.

A considerable crowd of sightseers hung about on the edge of the discussion, and David was able to press in among them.

Standing by the wall were the manager of the Arcadian, the assistant manager, and another official, whom David had never seen before, and, he was delighted to see, the man in the grey alpaca suit himself.

At close quarters, Saxon Marsh's grey emaciated face made an unpleasant impression upon the young man. Sir Leo, in his private opinion, was not a very formidable type of criminal. His heavy swashbuckling manner hid, David guessed, the proverbial cowardice of the bully.

But this man in the grey alpaca suit was a very different proposition. He was not a type but an individual, and in David's experience individuals, or people with strong personalities, were by no means easy to handle.

At the moment he was behaving in what David felt must be a characteristic fashion.

"My good sir," he was saying in his precise dry voice, "you misunderstand me. I am complaining. The stones on this path are uneven. Moreover, there is no shadow. The way the sun beats down upon this garden is a disgrace. Overcome by the heat, I stumbled over one of these infernal stones and only just saved myself from pitching over this ridiculously low wall to my death on the concrete below."

The manager, a fair, military-looking man with all his wits

about him, very different from the hysterical Mr. Populof of the Empress, regarded his client in shocked surprise.

"But, Mr. Marsh," he protested, and David made a note of the name, "I don't think you understand. A guest at this hotel has been very nearly killed. I'm sure you would wish to apologize for the terrible shock she has sustained. My dear sir, she might have died. Consider what might have happened then."

An unpleasant smile passed over Saxon Marsh's face.

"I think that is an eventuality which *you* have to consider," he said. "Not I. Both the lady and myself are the innocent victims of your disgraceful carelessness in permitting such old-fashioned monstrosities to remain in your garden."

The manager flushed, and David realized that the old man had scored his point. He knew enough about the law to realize that had Marguerite Ferney been killed and the case come into the coroner's court, this unpleasant old man, with the aid of a competent barrister, could have shifted the blame very neatly onto the hotel authorities. In fact, had it not been for that extraordinary recovery, which he himself had witnessed, he might almost have been inclined to believe the story himself.

"I'm very sorry about the lady," Marsh went on unctuously, adding placidly, "I'm afraid she has sustained considerable injury."

"No, I'm thankful to say not," said another man, evidently of the managerial staff, who had just joined the group. "I've been talking to the doctor. It's just shock. The urn didn't actually touch her at all. She had left her chair before the urn fell, and although she was borne to the ground by the crash, her injuries really don't amount to more than a few bruises. You're a very lucky man, Mr. Marsh."

"Not at all." Saxon Marsh's smile was grim, and David could have sworn that there was something which was disappointment, or even anger, in his eyes. "Not at all. I'm extremely glad the poor woman has met with no serious consequences of the accident, but I register a protest here and now. This hotel garden is dangerous and a menace. I shall write to *The Times* about it, or at any rate to the local county council. You may send me my bill."

Turning on his heel, he shouldered his way through the crowd and walked off, leaving them completely routed. David followed him with his eyes, and as he did so caught sight of the now familiar figure of Sir Leo Thyn hurrying across the grass to meet him.

The two met in the middle of the lawn, and Sir Leo turned back and walked to the hotel with his friend. David raised his eyebrows. So Sir Leo and Marsh did know each other. Now he was perfectly certain that the incident he had watched from his bedroom window had been no accident but a deliberate attempt to murder Marguerite Ferney in a diabolically clever way. David felt he was on the track at last.

10

FLIGHT

NOTHING at all."

Inspector Winn's brisk voice sounded positively dispirited over the telephone.

"He's vanished into thin air, Blest. I didn't think you'd have anything to report, but formal identification of the corpse has come through and I'm trying to pacify the chief constable as best I can. I put out a general call to the ports, so I expect we shall get him in the end. Thank you for phoning. Good-bye."

David hung up the receiver and walked out into the lounge of the Arcadian and, sitting down at a small table, ordered a lager. He was considerably troubled in his own mind about his own behaviour in regard to Winn's case. On the face of it he was holding back valuable information in order to shield Judy, but since his only informant on the subject of Birch's real identity was Bloomer, and Bloomer had since gone back on that evidence, he considered himself justified in not volunteering what might easily be a mare's nest.

He was sitting at his little table when Old Charlie came up to him. The old man was in garrulous mood.

"You'll see 'er come down in a minute," he murmured. "She

isn't half making a to-do. You'd think the whole hotel 'ad fallen on her and not a bunch of geraniums just missed her."

"Who? Miss Ferney?" said David, at last catching the thread of the old man's remarks.

"That's right." The waiter glanced speculatively across the lounge. "Doctors and nurses and specialists and a car, and I don't know what else. That's the sort of thing that doesn't do us any good. People never think of us, trying to make an honest living while the sun shines."

"So Miss Ferney's going, is she?" remarked David, anxious to keep the conversation going and excited by this new piece of information. "Where to?"

"That I couldn't say," said his informant with a strong suggestion that he did not care either. "To hospital, I should think. Or a private lunatic asylum per'aps. There's nothing wrong with her, sir, nothing wrong at all. Now, if the flower pot 'ad 'it 'er," he continued with grim relish, "that'd be a different story, that would. 'Ullo," he added, " 'ere they come. Right through the main 'all. As public as you please. Parading 'erself, that's what she's doing."

David glanced across the room as the lift slowly descended. The brass gates swung apart, and quite an important little procession emerged.

David was puzzled by the whole business. Marguerite Ferney had not struck him as the sort of person to make a fuss about nothing, but making a fuss she certainly was. She had disdained the manager's offer of a departure through a side door and had evidently insisted upon making her exit as public as possible.

Two black-coated figures emerged first; doctors, David supposed. And then Marguerite Ferney herself, looking pale and even more lovely than usual in a long buff coat of summer ermine. She was walking very unsteadily, supporting herself with an arm around the shoulders of two other women, one a little nurse whose face was completely hidden by the great folds of

Miss Ferney's enormous fur collar, the other a bigger, black-suited woman, obviously a lady's maid. Two hotel porters walked behind with masses of luggage.

It was really a very impressive exit, and David watched the slow progress of the group as they passed out of the foyer and down the steps into the enormous limousine which awaited them.

From where he sat David could just see the door of the car held open by a liveried chauffeur.

The maid entered first and drew her mistress in after her, while the nurse helped her from the pavement and finally slipped in after her.

There was something vaguely familiar about the turn of the girl's shoulders under the long blue cloak. David wondered where he had seen her before. But the thought slipped from his mind as the door slammed behind the girl and the car drove away.

He had been seated there for perhaps ten minutes after the car had gone when an extraordinary incident occurred. Sir Leo Thyn had rushed down the staircase and reached the desk before David noticed him, and it was his words, uttered in a shrill hysterical tone that cut through the buzz of conversation in the lounge, which first caught and held the young man's attention.

"Have you seen my ward, Miss Wellington? Has she gone out of here?"

David saw the desk clerk put out his hand to quiet the excitable old man, but Sir Leo repulsed the gesture.

"I tell you this is a question of life and death," he said, his voice rising in spite of himself.

David sprang to his feet and hurried over to the other man's side. As he came up he saw that Sir Leo's face was quivering with suppressed alarm and heard the question which he put so anxiously.

"Tell me, my man, you saw Miss Ferney leave this hotel. Was my ward with her? Tell me, yes or no?"

David stiffened. The nurse! The little turn of the shoulders that had been so vaguely familiar. He caught his breath.

"Yes, Sir Leo," he said, "she was. Tell me, what does it mean?"

Sir Leo turned upon him. He seemed suddenly to have become a very old man, and it dawned upon David that he hardly realized to whom he was speaking.

"It means," he said hoarsely, "that Miss Wellington is in danger, in danger of death."

The next moment recognition had leapt into his eyes, and he pulled himself together as best he could.

"Oh, Inspector, it's you, is it?" he said with a piteous attempt to speak normally. "You must forgive me. I am—er—a little put out. You mustn't pay attention to what I've been saying."

But David had seen the terror in his eyes and knew that for once in his life Sir Leo Thyn had spoken no less than the simple truth.

11

A FORTUNE AT STAKE

M Y DEAR MARGUERITE, you're a genius. The whole
thing has been done so neatly, so smoothly. I couldn't
have handled it better myself."

The man who spoke paused at the end of the chaise-longue
and looked down at the woman who lay upon it among a mass of
lace-covered cushions. After a moment's contemplation he
nodded approvingly.

Charles Carlton Webber, or Webb as he preferred to call
himself, was still in his early thirties. Of medium height, he was
spare and spruce, with a sharp-featured, clever face in which only
a certain narrowness about the eyes was in any way unpleasant.

Marguerite Ferney stirred languidly among her cushions and
smiled at him.

"Don't flatter yourself, darling," she said. "You wouldn't have
done it at all. This young woman is not at all the sort of kid to be
taken in by your fascinating manner. It was very fortunate that we
decided upon this way of handling it. We might have made a very
awkward mistake. She's an odd little person, simply absorbed in
her father, or her uncle Jim as she calls him. I shouldn't have had
any difficulty if it had been only her that I had to deal with, but it

wasn't easy with Sir Leo, to say nothing of a Scotland Yard man in attendance—an extraordinarily handsome young inspector, Charles. I quite lost my heart to him."

The man swung round upon her, a gleam of jealousy appearing in his eyes.

"What do you mean?"

Marguerite Ferney laughed. "Don't worry," she said. "I hardly spoke to him. My dear, I was much too busy to have any time for flirtation.

"You don't seem to realize," she went on, a faintly plaintive note creeping into her voice, "I've run a tremendous risk in bringing her here."

Webb smiled, and the narrowness of his eyes became more apparent.

"Are you afraid of Sir Leo?"

The faint sneer was not lost upon the woman, and her eyes flickered dangerously.

"Of Sir Leo, no," she said. "But of Saxon Marsh I think perhaps I am a little. You must realize, Charles, we're up against a very powerful enemy. There's something uncanny about that man, something terrifying. We must be very careful."

He came and sat down on the edge of the couch and took her hands in his.

"I'll be careful. Don't worry. I'm not a complete fool, Marguerite, whatever you think of me."

The room in which the two people sat was a long low apartment with big windows leading onto a balcony which overlooked a garden. At the end of the garden was a natural beach, over which the waves of the estuary swept every high tide.

In many ways it was an extraordinary place. Chalk cliffs rose on either side of the garden, and the house itself was built on a plateau of high ground set in a fold of the cliffs.

From where he sat Webb could look out over the balcony and see Judy walking about in the garden. She made a lonely, pathetic figure walking up and down among the flowering shrubs, her chin on her breast and her hands clasped behind her.

This fact was not lost upon the man.

"Rather a pretty kid," he remarked. "Oh, don't worry, my dear, she hasn't got your exotic beauty. But she's not a bad-looking little creature. It seems almost a pity, in view of everything."

Marguerite Ferney sat up sharply and with surprising vigour for one who was supposed to be suffering from acute nervous exhaustion.

"What do you mean? You're not going to do anything silly—anything dangerous—promise me! After all, remember I'm in this too. I brought her here, and I'm the legal beneficiary under the will. They'll go after me, not you. Oh, Charles, be careful, be careful."

He laughed at her fears but made no promise, a fact which the woman realized and was quick to seize upon.

Webb rose to his feet.

"Look here, Marguerite," he said. "I want you to realize that there's a fortune at stake. I've examined the will most carefully, and I know what I'm doing. If that girl out there is alive and married on the evening of her twenty-fourth birthday, that is to say in a few months' time, the whole of Silas Gillimot's fortune will go to her husband. If on that date she is alive but unmarried, she will receive a large income from the fortune, but the bulk of it will go to the heirs of Richard Ferney, your father."

He paused and laughed.

"Sir Silas, with his disapproval of women holding large sums of money in their own names, didn't think that your father's two elder sons might get wiped out in the same flying accident. I'm afraid he may turn in his grave, but we can't help that. The fact is, Marguerite, that you and I want that three hundred thousand pounds, or what there is left of it after that old embezzler, Sir Leo, has finished with it.

"And that's what I want to talk to you about," he went on

persuasively. "Three hundred thousand pounds! Think of it, Marguerite. Think of what it would mean to us: freedom from our creditors, and all the luxuries we both need and enjoy so much. I hope you're not going to let any silly scruples stand in my way or yours."

Marguerite Ferney rose from her couch. Her fair loveliness was enhanced by the long ivory lace robe which swathed her from head to foot.

She moved over to the window and looked down at Judy as the girl paced up and down the garden of the small natural fortress which enclosed her.

A faint twisted smile spread over the woman's lips.

"We must keep her hidden," she said. "We must keep her hidden until after her birthday. Surely it isn't difficult. With your ingenuity you can think of something."

Webb shook his head.

"It's no good, Marguerite. While you've been away I've been thinking it out. We don't want half a fortune, my dear. I imagine the original sum has been depleted considerably already. But that's not the point. This girl knows us now. If she came forward in a court of law and told her story at any future date, then there's a very reasonable chance that she might get away with it."

His voice trailed away, and the woman turned and looked at him.

"What are you suggesting?"

"I'm not suggesting," he said. "I've made up my mind. There's only one course which means absolute safety for us."

"And that?" she said faintly.

Webb smiled and looked out of the window.

"Our little friend must meet with some accident," he said. "Unfortunately fatal."

The woman stood very still. Every touch of colour had vanished from her face, and she stared at her companion, striving to read what lay behind the odd, masklike smile.

"No," she said suddenly. "No, you can't. It's too dangerous."

"That's where you're quite wrong, my dear," he said placidly. "Besides, don't bother your head about it. This is going to happen so simply and naturally that the police will be able to hold the fullest inquiries, if they wish to, without coming to any unpleasant conclusions."

He threw himself down in one of the big tapestry-covered easy chairs, and his smile was broad and complacent. Marguerite Ferney shuddered. She knew him in this mood. She was not a squeamish woman, but there were times when he appalled her.

Hers was not a moral objection. Marguerite was the last person in the world to worry about ethics. It was the risks he took, and the ruthlessness of his methods. She knew him for the man he was, a man for whom pity had no existence and for whom the affairs of other people had no meaning save where they crossed his own.

Meanwhile Judy Wellington walked idly round the garden and congratulated herself upon the turn events had taken. She dared not think of David, but apart from him and the thought of his worried, anxious face she felt happier than she had been for a considerable time.

The kindness of Marguerite Ferney took her breath away. All through the long drive in the big car, whose blinds had been drawn against the inquisitive glance of passers-by, Marguerite had been the soul of kindness itself, despite the fact that she was only just recovering from a terrible shock.

It did occur to the girl that she had no idea at all where she was or what was the name of the queer house with its extraordinary cliff-enclosed garden, but the fact held no alarm for her and she merely made a mental note to ask Marguerite at some future time.

She stood on the terrace and looked out beyond the beach and estuary to the lonely piece of mainland beyond. It was a very clear day, and she could just see the outlines of a single house among the greenery, but apart from that there seemed to be nothing but an expanse of grey-green marsh and salting.

She had been standing there, looking out across the dancing water, for some time when a light step behind her made her start and swing round.

Charles Webb stood behind her, the most charming of smiles upon his face.

"I'm so sorry if I startled you," he said, "but Marguerite wondered if you'd come up to her room. It's getting late, and it's rather cold out here. You must be very tired after your long journey."

He had a pleasant, easy way of talking, and an odd sort of familiarity which was not offensive.

"Why, yes, of course, I'll come up at once."

As they turned to go in he grinned at her.

"I'm afraid I ought to have introduced myself," he said. "I'm Marguerite's cousin. I keep an eye on her affairs. My name's Webb."

As they went into the house together he continued to chat, and Judy was bewildered and a little shy of him. In her innocence she summed him up as a pleasant, rather foolish person, probably not half so clever as he looked.

Marguerite was leaning back among her pillows as they entered, and now she stretched out her hand languidly towards the girl.

"Do sit down and make yourself as comfortable as you can. I do hope you don't mind: I've been talking about you to Charles. Oh, we can trust him absolutely," she added quickly as a scared expression crept into the girl's eyes. "He knows all my affairs. He studied medicine before he took up the law, and I've been talking to him about your illness. He's tremendously interested."

Judy looked uncomfortable. The time had come, she felt, to confess the truth to her new friends.

She told her story shyly, and they listened to her in silence, but although Charles laughed heartily when she confessed her deception, she had the uncomfortable feeling that Marguerite had not been wholly amused.

"I had to do it, you see," she said, "for Uncle Jim's sake. Uncle Jim couldn't bear me to be without him. And that's why I'm so anxious now. That's why I've jumped at your kind invitation. When do you think he'll be here?"

"Oh, quite soon now. My agent is in touch with him."

Marguerite spoke glibly. She had used Lionel Birch as a bait and had steeled herself to hear a good many such requests from the girl.

Judy shuddered. "Of course he didn't do it. I assured you of that in the beginning, didn't I? But I know he'll go anywhere to find me. He doesn't like me to be out of his sight even for a moment."

Charles Webb rose to his feet.

"It's all incredibly interesting," he said. "Do you mean to tell me that Sir Leo really believes that you're a permanent invalid?"

Judy nodded. "It's terrible, isn't it? But I'm afraid everybody at the Arcadian was convinced of it. You were completely taken in, weren't you, Marguerite?"

Marguerite Ferney hesitated.

"I thought you might not be quite so ill as you looked, my dear," she said at last, "but I had no idea that the whole thing was part of a carefully arranged plot. In fact, Charles, I must apologize," she went on, turning to him with a light laugh. "Your medical services won't be needed after all, you see."

"Oh, I don't know," he said. "I shan't despair." And although he spoke lightly there was an underlying note in his voice which made Judy look at him sharply, and for the first time some of the risk she was running in placing herself so entirely in her new friend's hands occurred to her.

After all, she had known Marguerite Ferney but a short time, and yet so great had been the other girl's charm that she had seen nothing extraordinary in her offer of assistance.

"We're all going to bed early," said Marguerite, breaking in upon her thoughts. "You look worn out, you poor child. I'll ring for Anna to take you to your room. It's rather a queer old house. You might not find it alone. You didn't mind having dinner on your own, did you?"

She stretched out her hand to the bell, but a sign from the man stopped her.

"Oh, don't send Miss Wellington away yet," he said. "I want to hear some more about this sham illness. It's quite the most extraordinary story I've ever heard. Tell me, Miss Wellington, there wasn't *anyone* except your uncle in your confidence? Wasn't there anyone, anyone at all?"

There was an odd urgency in his tone as he spoke, something that was not quite ordinary curiosity, but as Judy looked at him and saw the frank, open expression on his not unhandsome face she reproached herself for what seemed to be an altogether unwarrantable fit of nerves.

"No. No one at all," she said, and paused. She was going to say "except David," but thought better of it. After all, the story would need some explanation, and she did not want to be forced into talking about David or even thinking about him. Even now she was regretting that she had not trusted him more thoroughly.

"Well, that's amazing," Webb said softly. "Everyone at the Arcadian, waiters, chambermaids, bellboys, lift attendants, everyone, as well as your guardian, believe you to have been a permanent invalid. Tell me, Miss Wellington, did you discuss your malady with anybody? Forgive my interest, but it's such a wonderful hoax for you to have played upon everyone."

Judy flushed. There was an odd brightness in his eyes which she did not quite like and was at a loss to understand. He saw her hesitation and hurried on.

"But of course you didn't," he said. "Why should you? But tell me, what form did this remarkable malady take?"

Judy blushed. "Oh, I don't know," she said. "I was just very pale and weak. It seemed to work all right."

"But naturally, it would. How extremely clever of you! Well, Miss Wellington, Marguerite's right: you must be absolutely worn out after your excitements of the day."

Marguerite rang the bell, and Judy looked at her. The woman read the unspoken question in the girl's eyes and held out her hand.

"My dear child," she said, "don't worry. We'll get hold of your uncle, and you can both have sanctuary here for as long as you like. This is an out-of-the-way place. If the worst comes to the worst it's quite a little fortress. You go to bed now and sleep, and in the morning I shall have good news for you, I'm certain of it."

Judy's eyes grew big with gratitude.

"Oh, Marguerite, you're a darling," she said, and kissed the woman impulsively.

Marguerite Ferney sat very stiff and straight in her nest of cushions, and Judy, looking at her, wondered why the beautiful face should assume such a mask of pallor at the caress.

Anna, the big, rather grim-faced woman who had accompanied them on their flight from the Arcadian, conducted her to her bedroom. She had not been taken to the room on her first arrival, and now was rather surprised to find it a smallish room on the top floor of the house, which was, although very comfortably furnished, oddly cold and uninviting.

"Here you are, miss. I think you'll be comfortable here. I've unpacked your things and put them away in the cupboard, as I imagine you'll be staying some little time."

The maid spoke in an odd expressionless voice, and although she smiled at the girl there was nothing sincere about her, and she moved and spoke, Judy thought, as though she were an automaton.

She went out, and the girl was left alone. As she undressed and prepared for bed it occurred to Judy that the thing which made the room so uninviting was the fact that the window was set rather high in the wall. The room had been a nursery at some time, she decided, for there were thin but very firm iron bars across it on the outside.

She had pulled back the curtains and was standing staring out across the sea, now just a grey mist in the dusk, when there was a tap on her door, and the maid Anna reappeared.

"Miss Marguerite has sent you a cup of tea, miss," she said. "She always takes it herself just before going to bed and thought you might care to have some."

Judy thanked the woman. Although it was high summer, the evening was chill, and the hot tea was inviting.

Anna set the tray down on the bedside table and began to fold up Judy's discarded clothes for her.

As she sipped the tea the girl watched the woman at work and reflected that it must be very pleasant to be wealthy enough to have a lady's maid to look after one: rather like having a nurse again, she decided.

The tea was very strong and tasted almost bitter, and although Judy added a considerable amount of cream from the little silver pitcher, it did not seem to lose its odd, distinctive flavour.

She caught Anna looking at her thoughtfully as she set down the pitcher.

"I'm sorry if it's a bit strong, miss," she said. "I'm afraid you don't like it."

Judy was quick to sense the note of disappointment in her voice and was anxious not to hurt her feelings.

"It's perfectly all right, Anna," she said, gulping down the remainder of the liquid. "Thank you so much for bringing it."

She set the cup down upon the tray, and the woman hurried over and, picking it up, bade her a hasty good-night.

Her departure was so rapid that Judy was astonished. She

turned towards the bed, and as she did so was conscious for the first time of a queer numb sensation which seemed to be spreading rapidly over her. Her senses reeled. The outlines of the furniture became blurred and indistinct. She felt drowsy and as though every bone in her body had suddenly become made of lead.

A great fear seized her. Even her thoughts were becoming confused, but she remembered the tea and the odd bitter taste in it.

By sheer force of will she dragged herself towards the door. Her fingers closed upon the handle. The weight of her limbs was dragging her down, and the insufferable drowsiness was becoming more irresistible at every moment.

She turned the handle and pulled, only to meet resistance. In her terror she threw off for a moment the powerful narcotic drug and tugged at the door with all her strength, but the wood remained firmly in place, and with her last conscious thought she realized that it was locked and she was a prisoner.

1 2

THE ANGRY MAN

I 'M FINISHED, MARSH. I can't go on any longer. This is
more than I can stand."

Few people would have recognized Sir Leo Thyn in the man
who stood trembling before the great desk at which Saxon Marsh
was seated.

Any doctor would have pronounced him in urgent need of
medical treatment. His nerves had gone completely, and it was a
trembling, shrunken old man who stood cowering in his friend's
luxurious suite.

"We shall lose everything. We're beaten, Marsh. Our only
chance is to lay hands on all we've got and clear out of the
country."

Saxon Marsh did not appear to hear. He was writing, and only
an increased pallor in his cheeks betrayed any uneasiness in his
state of mind.

There was silence in the room, broken only by the scratching
of his pen.

Sir Leo brought his fist down with a crash upon the desk.

"Listen to me," he said. "It's our only chance. We must clear
out. I shall go to Greece. I've got enough money to live there

quietly, for a time, at least. Are you coming with me, or must I go alone?"

Saxon Marsh raised his head slowly, and for a long moment his cavernous eyes rested upon the other man's face. Then he pressed a bell, and immediately a secretary entered.

Marsh spoke without glancing at him.

"Has Johnson returned?"

"Yes, Mr. Marsh. Here is the message."

The secretary laid an envelope on the table and went out quickly. All Saxon Marsh's employees seemed to share his own strange inhuman quality.

Saxon Marsh tore open the envelope, glanced at the contents, and then, opening a drawer in the desk, took out a sheet of paper.

"There, Thyn," he said. "In this envelope is a first-class ticket which will see you as far as Marseilles. There are also five one-hundred-pound notes for immediate expenses. Sign this paper and they're yours. Any of my secretaries is trustworthy, and you can arrange with one of them, or with your own man, to have your own private fortune transferred to a bank out there."

Thyn took up the paper with a trembling hand. For some minutes he studied its contents. Then it dropped from his fingers and fluttered down upon the polished wood of the desk.

"This empowers you to take full charge of the Gillimot fortune," he said. "Good heavens, man, do you realize what you're doing?"

Saxon Marsh shrugged his thin shoulders.

"Certainly," he said. "I'm assuming your responsibilities. In other words, you're stepping out, and I'm taking over. Don't imagine, my dear Thyn, that I'm going to pull this thing off for you to step in afterwards and share the profits. Either you stay and play your part or you leave it entirely to me."

A travesty of a smile passed over Sir Leo's face.

"This is a legal document," he said. "You must have had it prepared for some days."

"I admit the eventuality had occurred to me," said Marsh, "and I was prepared for it. Make up your mind, though."

"If I refuse?"

Marsh refused. "I don't think you will. You're frightened. Only a moment ago you were urging me to run away. Now you're afraid of your own suggestion. If you think we're going to fail, now's your chance to get out. If you don't, stay behind and take the risk."

A discreet tap on the door interrupted the conversation, and the same secretary entered. He laid a slip of paper on the table and went out again. Marsh glanced at it and tossed it over. It was a memorandum slip containing the cryptic message:

D. B. has returned from interviewing landlady at chauffeur's lodgings. Appears to have learned nothing.

Saxon Marsh smiled.

"Our inspector is getting worried," he said. "A very tenacious man, Thyn. He should be working for us. Ever since you made your idiotic mistake of blabbing out your fears to him he has been working like a fiend in his attempt to get hold of Marguerite Ferney's whereabouts. I shall let him try a little longer. After all, he may find something of use. Policemen sometimes do."

He laid a peculiar emphasis upon the word "policemen," and Sir Leo gulped.

"It's madness," he said hoarsely. "It's madness to stay. The game's up, Marsh. Why not admit it?"

Saxon Marsh dipped a pen into the ink and handed it to his erstwhile friend.

Sir Leo hesitated and was lost. He seized the pen and scribbled his name at the foot of the document.

Without a word the other man took it from his trembling hand and passed him the envelope.

"Bon voyage, my friend," he said, smiling.

Sir Leo turned back, his face convulsed with rage.

"I believe you're double-crossing me," he said.

Saxon Marsh drew out the document the other had just signed.

"Suppose we tear it up?" he suggested. "I'm quite prepared. Only make up your mind; there's no time to lose. If our young friend is not rescued from the amiable Marguerite Ferney I may wish that I had taken your advice. And there is also the young inspector to consider. Hurry, man, hurry. There's work to be done."

Sir Leo drew back from the desk.

"I'll go," he said. "I'll go. I can't stand it any longer." And without once looking behind him he strode out of the room.

Saxon Marsh looked after him. Then a smile spread over his face, and, after a few seconds had elapsed, his long thin hand reached out and touched a bell.

The subservient secretary was with him in a moment.

"Has Johnson gone?" Saxon Marsh's voice was unusually soft.

"Yes, sir. He's followed Sir Leo."

"Good, good." As though to give more force to the monosyllable, Saxon Marsh nodded on the word. "That's right, Marshall. You may go, but don't forget to keep me informed at every step."

The young secretary opened his mouth as though he would ask a question, but the expression in his employer's eyes silenced him, and he moved noiselessly out of the room.

Left alone, Saxon Marsh leant back in his chair and smiled. For some time he seemed lost in contemplation of singularly happy thoughts, but gradually the smile vanished from his face as a new expression took its place, and in that moment Saxon Marsh looked a very formidable enemy, a fit match indeed for Charles Carlton Webb.

At the precise moment that Saxon Marsh sat contemplating the flight of his partner, Sir Leo Thyn, Inspector David Blest was engaged in doing what no policeman should ever think of attempting, even in cases of considerable emergency. He was breaking into a hotel room.

It was nine o'clock in the evening, and the upper floors of the hotel were deserted. Even the chambermaids were off duty, and the time was admirably suited to his project.

Marguerite Ferney had occupied a suite of three rooms on the third floor, and when David had succeeded in effecting an entrance by means of a piece of bent wire manipulated with a dexterity which would not have disgraced a professional cracksman, he found himself in a sitting room which still smelt faintly of an exotic perfume and which still bore traces of its recent occupation.

David knew quite well what he was doing and had decided to take the risk. The one thing firmly fixed in his mind was the fact that Judy was in danger and that she must be discovered at all costs.

He set about his task with that methodical thoroughness which is the outcome of a Yard training. He searched all three rooms, moving slowly through them without appearing to hurry in the least, and yet with an odd precision and a meticulous tidiness.

Every scrap of paper was examined, every drawer pulled out, every cupboard door opened, every corner and waste-paper basket turned over.

The maid's room and Miss Ferney's own luxurious bedroom yielded nothing which could be considered a clue, unless the empty perfume bottle labelled "Vérité, Rue des Marchands, Paris" could be said to be one.

Looking at it, David was inclined to think not. After all, Vérité's was a large concern, and it was unlikely that they would remember the name and address of the person who had bought the bottle, even were there sufficient time to ask them.

He went on with his search, steadily growing more and more despondent, and the sick feeling of alarm for Judy overpowering him.

And then, just as he was giving up hope, he made a discovery.

In the bottom of a waste-paper basket in the sitting room he found a torn half sheet of blotting paper. He spread it out upon the little escritoire in front of the window and examined it carefully.

At first he thought it was going to profit him nothing. The centre of the page was an undecipherable mass of blottings, and he was about to throw it away disconsolately when something caught his eye, and he held the paper closer to the light.

Then an exclamation of satisfaction escaped him. Embedded in the thick, soft paper was the indentation of words evidently written with a hard pencil on a thin sheet of paper placed over it.

Gradually he made out some of them, and his satisfaction grew. It was a list of towns, evidently scribbled down in a woman's hand, and David's heart leapt as he deciphered them.

He made out "East Bay," which he knew to be some ten miles from Westbourne, and then "Greydean," a small township some few miles farther on in an easterly direction.

With a thrill of delight he realized his good fortune. He had discovered the route Marguerite Ferney had planned, to give to her chauffeur.

Folding the precious slip of paper in his wallet, he let himself out of the suite and went noiselessly down to his own room to complete his task. It was not easy.

Towards the end of the list the towns became illegible, and finally in despair he went down to the bureau for a road map and a gazetteer.

Here he found a snag. The clerk, although smiling and polite, firmly refused to allow him to take the volumes up to his room, but hospitably offered him the use of the office for so long as he should need it.

David made the best of a bad job. He was in a hurry. Moreover, there seemed no particular need for secrecy. Rather more from habit than deliberate intention, he kept the overfriendly little clerk at arm's length. But the man appeared to be bored, and whenever David looked up he saw his watery blue eyes fixed inquisitively upon the list he was making.

Half an hour's work left David with the information that Marguerite Ferney's list of towns had ended, so far as he could tell, at Hintlesham in Kent, but he had no means of telling if the journey ended at that point or if it merely indicated that the chauffeur knew his way from that spot.

He wrote the name down upon his list and sat looking at it thoughtfully, his mind very far away from the inquisitive clerk whose would-be casual glance was directed upon the paper in front of him.

Finally David rose, and with a word of thanks hurried out into the lounge. He knew well that he might be setting out upon a wild-goose chase, but on the other hand it seemed most unlikely that Marguerite Ferney would map out a route which she did not intend to take, and Judy was in danger.

He glanced at his watch. By hard driving through the night he guessed he might reach Hintlesham by six in the morning. The only thing which prevented him setting out at once was a certain guilty feeling concerning his duty to Inspector Winn. It was true that he only held a watching brief, as it were, in the Johnny Deane case, and that Winn was doing his best to freeze him out, but the fact remained that he was engaged on the job.

He glanced again at the list he had made out. The temptation was very strong.

It was at this moment that he felt a touch upon his arm. Swinging round, he caught sight of the little watery-eyed clerk again. The man seemed to be excited.

"You're Inspector Blest, aren't you, sir? I thought so. There's a telephone call for you. It seems to be urgent. The name is Colonel Cream, sir. Will you take it in my office? You'll be undisturbed there."

David followed the man back into the little room and picked up the telephone receiver.

"Hallo, is that you, Blest, my boy?" the chief constable's voice sounded far off and indistinct. "This is a confounded line," the voice continued. "I can hardly hear you. Now, listen. I've got private information that the Northampton police are holding a man on a motoring offence. His description tallies with Birch exactly. I want you to go up there tonight. Have you got a car? Oh, splendid. Well, look, go at once, and don't tell anyone."

"Don't tell anyone, sir?" David's voice betrayed his astonishment.

He heard a smothered explosion at the other end of the wire.

"Don't tell Winn," said the chief constable. "This is completely unofficial, you understand. But I think they've got the man, and I want you to bring him in. I can rely on you to do that, can't I, as a personal favour to me?"

He rang off, and David hung up the receiver very slowly. The whole business was extraordinarily unorthodox, but from what he had seen of Colonel Cream that did not surprise him.

Policemen like Inspector Winn may easily be unpopular with their own chief constable.

He went slowly out again. There was nothing for it. His long training told him that he must obey the Colonel implicitly. He was not a free agent.

The clue he held to Judy's whereabouts was slender indeed. A comforting thought occurred to him. If the man at Northampton was indeed Lionel Birch, alias Jim Wellington, then he was more likely to be able to tell him about Marguerite Ferney than anyone else in the world.

He collected his driving coat and made for his battered but reliable car.

Up in his room Saxon Marsh sat peering at the little watery-eyed clerk who stood quaking before him.

"Yes, sir. Hintlesham, sir," he was saying. "I saw it with my own eyes. Hintlesham in Kent."

Saxon Marsh hesitated. It was on the tip of his tongue to ask if the young policeman had appeared impressed by his masterly imitation of his old acquaintance, Colonel Cream; but Saxon Marsh was above everything discreet, and contented himself with a nod to the clerk and a word to his secretary to fetch his coat and order his car.

13

POLICE NET

DAVID SPED OUT of Westbourne, his ancient but still reliable car settling into her stride for the night's journey.

On the corner of Head Street, where the bright lights of the town give place to the suburbs, he passed the police headquarters, and the pressure of his foot on the accelerator wavered for an instant in response to an impulse to pause and look in on Inspector Winn.

The big uncurtained windows of his office on the second floor were wide, for the night was very warm. The lights were blazing as David glanced up, and he all but changed his mind and called in.

However, he recollected the length of his journey and the peculiar request for secrecy which the eccentric chief constable had impressed upon him, and, leaving police headquarters behind, he sped on into the darkness just as Saxon Marsh had intended him to.

Meanwhile, the scene in the big airy police office was one so interesting that it was a thousand pities that he had missed it.

Inspector Winn, spruce, sharp-witted, and unfriendly, sat behind his large flat-topped desk. Behind him a young constable, hot but stolid-looking, sat writing at a table in a corner, his helmetless head bent over his work.

Yet another constable, bland and exceedingly square, stood across the doorway, while Sergeant McCabe, a large, sensible person with mild eyes and enormous hands and feet, stood on the hearthrug.

McCabe was Winn's immediate subordinate, and like his superior officer was considerably excited and exasperated by the Deane case.

One civilian, a visitor to this odd police party, lounged in a chair which had been set for him in the very centre of the room, directly opposite the inspector's desk.

He was not altogether a prepossessing person, being slight, fair, and insignificant of feature, but at the moment he was very pleased with himself and there was a self-satisfied smirk on his peaky face, while his round black eyes were bright and inquisitive as a sparrow's.

It was not often that Nifty Martin found himself visiting a police station of his own free will. He was finding it a delightful experience. He had evidently dressed up for the occasion, and his white flannels, if cheap and somewhat fanciful in cut, were at least new and speckless.

He leant back in the chair, his pointed tan-and-white shoes very much in evidence.

But if Inspector Winn was impressed by these sartorial details he did not show it.

"Look here, Martin," he said, "doesn't it occur to you that we might think it rather odd that you should keep quiet for twenty-four hours before you come forward with any of this precious information of yours? Why didn't you come down to see us immediately?"

Nifty Martin looked aggrieved.

"I've got me own sweet life to live, Inspector," he remarked, "without taking on other people's jobs. I wouldn't be here now if I hadn't been such a friend of the Major's. Known each other for years, we had. I was quite cut up when I heard he was dead."

Winn was contemptuous. "Very touching, I'm sure," he said. "I suppose you both graduated from Borstal in the same year? But that won't cut any ice with me. You came here because you hoped to get a reward, and if you put us on the right track I don't say you won't get one. But if you've got anything to say, out with it, and the sooner the better."

Nifty Martin rose to his feet, picked up his straw boater, and turned towards the door. The bland constable did not move, and Winn's voice rapped out like a gunshot:

"Don't be a fool, Martin. Sit down. You've come here to tell your story, and you're not going until you do."

Nifty Martin hesitated, but he was a small man, and the room was full of policemen. He fell back on sarcasm.

"Nice lot you are," he said. "So friendly. So reasonable. When a fellow comes round here with a really useful piece of information, something that'll save you weeks and weeks of work, how d'you treat him? Like a blinking lord, I don't think. The way you're treating me you'd think you'd dragged me in, not I'd come up to you on a friendly visit to give you the lowdown about the death of an old pal."

Inspector Winn sighed. But if he was a hasty man he was not a complete fool, and he had had some experience of gentlemen of Nifty Martin's type.

"I assure you we appreciate all you're doing, Martin," he said gruffly.

The little man permitted a gratified smile to pass over his face. "Well," he said, "first of all, you're on the wrong track completely. You've got your bloodhounds out after the wrong man. You think it was Lionel Birch who did the Major in. Well, let me tell you, you're wrong. It wasn't, see? I happen to know."

"Indeed?" Winn drawled. "How do you know so much about it?"

Nifty Martin shrugged his shoulders.

"Unbelieving lot, aren't you?" he said. "I happen to know because I saw everything—or nearly everything."

There was a smothered exclamation from Sergeant McCabe, and Winn leant forward.

"Do you mean to tell me you were in the room?" he demanded.

"In the room? Oh dear me no!" Nifty laughed. "If I 'adn't got a perfect alibi I wouldn't be sitting 'ere. I'm not barmy. I know enough about the police to expect them to be suspicious. I was in a room on the opposite side of the street, and there's two or three people who can bear witness that I was there the whole evening. I was kneeling on a couch, leaning on the windowsill in me shirt-sleeves, like any other gentleman at the seaside."

McCabe stepped forward and murmured a word or two in Winn's ear. A few scattered phrases were audible.

"That little boarding house in White Horse Alley . . . runs along behind the hotel . . . alibi verified."

Winn nodded testily, and the sergeant withdrew.

It was quite obvious to Winn that Nifty himself could have had nothing to do with the murder, or wild horses would not have forced him to come forward unasked.

The inspector cleared his throat noisily.

"All this you tell me is extraordinarily interesting, Martin," he said. "Suppose you make yourself quite clear. You say you were leaning out of the window in your boarding house behind the hotel all the evening? What do you mean by that?"

"Well, I was there from nine o'clock until about midnight. Ask my landlady. Ask her daughter. Ask any of 'em."

"I will," Winn promised. "Did you see Johnny Deane shot?"

Nifty hesitated. "Well, I did and I didn't," he said at last. "I'll tell you about it. I'd come down to see Johnny, and there were reasons why we couldn't stay at the same hotel. We were quite friendly, mind. It was just that he had a bit of business on hand, and I promised to keep out of the way although near enough if I was needed, if you see what I mean."

A grim smile spread over the sergeant's face, and even Inspector Winn looked down at the papers on his desk. It was evident that Nifty Martin did not wish to go into too many details, and as policemen they could guess what his reasons were.

"Well, I stayed at the boarding house, and I chose a room that overlooked Johnny's," said Nifty, gratified that the most awkward part of his story had gone by without question. "On the night that he was killed Johnny was going out to see the man he was doing a bit of business with, and he said to me, 'I don't like it, Nifty. I've a good mind to throw in me hand.' I said to him, 'Don't do anything rash, Johnny,' but he wouldn't listen to me, and all he said was, 'You wait up at the window, and when you see me come in I'll signal to you how things are going, and perhaps we'll meet out somewhere for a drink.' "

An incredulous expression came into the inspector's eyes.

"Do you mean to tell me that you waited at your window from nine o'clock until midnight in the hope of Johnny Deane signalling to you to come out for a drink?" he demanded. "Are you sure you're not just wasting our time?"

"Wait a minute, wait a minute! Let me get me story out." Nifty was annoyed. "I wasn't only waiting for Johnny, if you must know. I was keeping an eye on a gentleman that Johnny was interested in. The same gentleman that's interested you lately. Mr. Lionel Birch, 'e called 'imself. Johnny wanted me to let 'im know if the old boy was in 'is room when Johnny came back, because 'e wanted to have a word with 'im."

Winn turned round and looked up at the sergeant, and the two men exchanged meaning glances. Lionel Birch was fitting into the puzzle at last.

"Well, I waited," Nifty continued. "I waited until close on eleven o'clock, and then I saw Mr. Lionel Birch go into 'is room. It wasn't so very far off Johnny's own room, although there was some difference in the numbering, I understand. Anyway, I could just see into it by leaning right out of my window. Fortunately the old boy liked fresh air and kept 'is curtains back and 'is window wide, like you do 'ere, Inspector.

"Well, let me tell you this: Mr. Lionel Birch entered 'is room before Johnny came into 'is, and what's more 'e didn't go out of it, because I watched 'im get into bed and lie there readin'. He didn't seem to realize that 'is room was overlooked from this side of the street, or perhaps 'e never thought about it."

Winn cut in upon him.

"Of course we've only got your word for this, haven't we?" he said.

"Only mine and me landlady's," said Nifty. "Still," he went on impudently, "I won't give evidence if you don't want me to. I'm only trying to put you on the right track, and if it's the track I know it is, you're going to sit up before I've done."

In the ordinary way Inspector Winn might have lost interest at this point in the proceedings, but there was something peculiarly interesting in the little man's voice, and there was a gleam of real shrewdness in the sharp, birdlike eyes.

"Did you see Deane come into his room?" Winn demanded.

Nifty met his eyes. "Yes, I did," he said. "He came over to the window and signalled to me to wait for a minute. I thought he meant he was coming round to see me, but as I hung there watching I saw him pull his suitcase out from under the bed and start throwing his clothes into it. I didn't have a very clear view because of the dressing table set across the window in his room, but I could see bits of 'im, if you follow my meaning.

"After a minute or two, while I was standing there watching, I saw 'im leave the suitcase and go over to the door—at least, I imagined it was to the door, I couldn't actually see it. Then I saw 'im backing slowly with 'is 'ands 'eld over 'is head. Then 'e disappeared—dropped down out o' sight. There wasn't a sound. The fellow used a silencer, I suppose."

"Did you see the other man?"

"Not too clearly. Only bits of 'im, as I tell you."

There was no doubt that the man was telling the truth, and the policemen were impressed in spite of themselves.

"I'll tell you one thing, though," Nifty continued. "Whoever it was, it wasn't Lionel Birch,"

"How do you know that?" Winn's tone was positively belligerent.

"Because I could see 'im," said Nifty Martin. "I could see 'im, lying in bed reading, like I told you."

Winn leant back. "Doesn't it strike you as being extraordinary, if your story is true, Martin, that you didn't rush round to see what had happened to your friend?"

Nifty Martin met the other man's eyes squarely.

"Since my story *is* true, Inspector," he said, "it doesn't strike me as being extraordinary at all. Nor it won't you, if you think a minute."

Sergeant McCabe coughed loudly. Nifty had scored a point. Winn leant back in his chair.

"Constable," he said to the man at the door, "is that girl Ruth Dartle downstairs?"

"Yes, sir. She came over at once when the sergeant phoned through that you wanted to speak to her."

"Will you bring her up here, then?"

While the man was gone the inspector returned to Nifty.

"As soon as you arrived and told the sergeant that you had a story which might clear Birch I sent for this girl," he said. "I'd like you to hear what she has to say."

"Happy, I'm sure," said Nifty under his breath.

Miss Dartle came in looking even more untidy in her best clothes than in her dressing gown. She was breathless with apprehension and seemed to be in terror that she would be locked up on the spot.

Inspector Winn rose and escorted her to a chair. He fancied he knew how to manage awkward witnesses.

"Miss Dartle," he said, "it was so good of you to come. I wonder if you'd just repeat the evidence you so kindly gave us last night. It was just before eleven o'clock, if you remember."

The girl moistened her dry lips with the tip of her tongue.

"That's right," she said. "Just before eleven o'clock Mr. Lionel Birch met me in the passage at the hotel and asked me the way to Mr. Deane's room. I'll swear that, sir."

A slow smile spread over Winn's face, and he glanced at Nifty.

"How does that fit in with your story, Martin?" he said. "As far as I can gather from you, Lionel Birch was in his room from half-past ten until after the crime had been committed."

"So he was," said Nifty.

"Are you suggesting Miss Dartle is telling an untruth?"

Nifty shrugged his shoulders. "I'd like to ask 'er one question," he said. "That's all."

"Fire away."

Nifty turned and surveyed the girl slowly.

"Was he in fancy dress, young woman?" he said unexpectedly.

She stared at him.

"Well, yes, of course he was," she said. "I told you so, Mister Inspector, didn't I?"

"You did not," said Winn dryly. "What sort of fancy dress?"

Miss Dartle was quite upset. She burst into tears.

"I was sure I'd told you, and I don't think it matters anyway. It was a long black dressing-gown thing with a hood. He quite frightened me coming up in the dark passage. I said to 'im that 'e did."

Winn sighed heavily.

"Suppose you tell me exactly what he said and exactly what you said, as far as you can remember it."

After some pressing Miss Dartle did as she was requested.

"I said, 'Oh sir, you frightened me with that 'ood up,' and 'e said, 'I'm sorry. I've just been to a dance at the Arcadian. Didn't you recognize me? I'm in room fifty.' And I said, 'Oh, Mr. Birch, isn't it?' and he said, 'Yes. Can you direct me to Major Deane's room? He's an old friend of mine.' And I said, 'It's just along there—number seventy-three, sir,' and that's all I remember. Oh dear, have I done anything wrong?"

Some few minutes later, when Sergeant McCabe had conducted the weeping Miss Dartle downstairs, Winn turned to Nifty.

"I suppose you're going to tell me that the man you saw through the window in Deane's room was in fancy dress?" he said.

"He had a long black coat affair over his evening clothes," said Nifty cautiously. "They call 'em dominoes, don't they? Worn by people who want to join the party but aren't sporting enough to dress up as Father Christmas."

Inspector Winn shook his head. "It's no good, Martin," he said. "Everything you've told us is very interesting, but it's not evidence, you know."

"All right. Have it your own way."

Once again Nifty picked up his hat, but again the inspector motioned him to be seated.

"Wait a minute," he said. "I just want to check this. You say that you're prepared to swear that Lionel Birch was in his room at the same time as Deane was interviewing another man in his bedroom farther along the landing?"

"That's about it." Nifty seemed very sure of himself. "It's not only my word, remember. There was another person, my land-lady, looking out of the window at the same time as I was."

Winn laid down his pencil and looked at the other man steadily.

"Now, Martin," he said, "suppose we come to hard facts. What prompted you to come here tonight? I suppose you're going to tell me that you're a conscientious citizen who likes to see justice done? Well, I'm afraid that's not going to wash. You've got a grudge against someone. That's why you're here. What is it? Out with it."

Nifty laughed. "My word, aren't you clever!" he said derisively. "Smart as paint, you are. You can read the thoughts in the back of a bloke's mind. . . . 'The Man with the X-Ray Eyes.' "

Winn flushed. It was very difficult to put up with this sort of impudence in front of members of his own staff. Nifty was in an unassailable position, however, and the little man knew it.

"Well, you're wrong," he said. "I haven't come here out of spite. But Johnny was a pal of mine, and, believe it or not, I don't like to see a fellow getting away with murder just because 'e's wealthy and because 'e's got a handle to 'is name. That's why I'm here. Not but what if there's a reward going I wouldn't take it," he added somewhat hastily.

"Who are you talking about?" said Winn, his curiosity aroused. "You can speak freely, but don't forget that any unfounded accusations may rebound back on your own head."

Nifty leant forward in his chair.

"Johnny came down here because 'e was going to do a confidential job for a very wealthy old gent.

It wasn't the ordinary sort of job, but something very secret. Johnny wouldn't tell me what it was, but I know 'e thought there was something fishy about it, and it was dangerous.

"Yesterday 'e got the wind up proper and told the old bloke that 'e was going to walk out on 'im—at least, I think 'e told 'im; I know 'e meant to. I don't know what you think, Inspector, but doesn't it strike you as being queer that when 'e came back from that interview someone followed 'im into 'is room at the hotel and shot 'im with a gun that had a silencer?"

Winn did not reply directly to the question. Instead he asked another.

Nifty hesitated.

"Suppose I do tell you 'is name," he said, "what then?"

"You'll have to trust us to see that any reward that's going comes your way."

"Just my luck," said Nifty. "Still, since I've gone so far I'll go the whole hog."

And leaning forward he mentioned clearly and unmistakably the last name in the world Inspector Winn expected to hear.

"*Sir Leo Thyn?*" Winn was incredulous. "You're off your head."

Nifty waited for the storm to subside. Then he pulled a crumpled piece of paper out of his pocket.

"Take a look at that," he said.

The inspector glanced at the scribbled words.

DEAR MAJOR DEANE,

I am now setting out for the Arcadian. If you will meet me there a little before five o'clock I shall be very pleased. Yours faithfully,

LEO THYN.

"That came for Johnny yesterday," said Nifty. "He threw it away, and I picked it up. However," he said, a curiously malicious light creeping into his narrow eyes, "if you don't believe me, why not have a word or two with Sir Leo, all friendly like? He's staying at the Arcadian. Ring him up."

Inspector Winn did not seem to have heard this suggestion, but after a moment or two of consideration he drew the tele-phone towards him and had a few words with Sergeant McCabe downstairs.

As he hung up the receiver after issuing his instructions he turned to Nifty.

"Well, there you are, my lad," he said. "And if you're trying to make fools of us you know what's coming to you."

It was nearly ten minutes later when Sergeant McCabe came hurrying into the office. He murmured a few words to his superior, and Nifty had the satisfaction of seeing an expression of blank incredulity spread over the inspector's face.

"Gone?" said Winn. "Gone? What do you mean—gone?"

"Well, he's hopped it, sir. Left for the Continent in a hurry. We might catch him at Dover. Shall I try?"

Inspector Winn did not answer immediately. Blank astonishment, disbelief, and alarm were all visible in his expression.

"But why did Lionel Birch bunk?" he demanded of the room at large. "Why was his room dismantled, and where in the name of good fortune is he now?"

There was a long pause, during which Nifty Martin stirred happily and smiled at the tips of his impossible shoes.

"Go on," he said, "you can search me."

14

JOURNEY BY NIGHT

AN HOUR BEFORE DAWN David Blest found himself driving down the long straight road between Kraven and Witchingham. The road is one of the loneliest in England, running as it does through the wooded estates of Witchingham Parva and Kraven Common.

It was an eerie place even in daytime, with its high over-hanging trees and steep banks on either side of the road.

He had gone some four miles down the famous ten-mile stretch when for the first time certain misgivings assailed him. It was odd, he reflected, that there was no other road to Witching-ham, and yet at this time of night it was completely and utterly deserted.

Suddenly an alarming idea occurred to him. In his anxiety about Judy he had not considered his own position too carefully, but now it came home to him that it was very extraordinary that Colonel Cream should send him out on a night journey which would take him across this lonely strip of road, after warning him not to communicate with Inspector Winn.

David slowed the car down and cursed himself for a fool. He pulled himself together, however. After all, why should he expect a trap? David had a great faith in the inviolability of the law, and there were few criminals, in his opinion, who would risk a deliberate and planned attack on a Scotland Yard man. The police were notoriously hard on such cases, and very few attacks on policemen went unavenged.

All the same, he had made up his mind not to stop for anyone, and whipping up the car to its full speed he shot down the tunnel of trees at a great rate.

He was just reproaching himself for being unnecessarily jumpy when the unexpected occurred. Giant headlights were switched on at the side of the road, and in their glare he made out the figure of a man gesticulating wildly to him to stop.

David ignored him, put his foot hard down on the accelerator and, keeping his eyes on the near side edge of the road, roared past.

It was a tricky business, for the light was straight in his eyes and well-nigh blinding. However, he kept the old car on the road and thought he had got clear, but a moment later his car seemed to gather up all her wheels and take a flying leap at the ditch, while the shrill ping of a revolver bullet was drowned in the much larger explosion made by the bursting of his back tire.

All David's efforts to right the car were unavailing. She charged the soft grass-grown bank, churned into the earth, coughed, and stood still.

David whipped out his gun and waited. There were footsteps on the road; four or five men running, he judged, and he sat there waiting until they should come.

His vigil was not long drawn out. The first thing he knew was the splatter of a revolver bullet across the window. He fired back and thought he heard a gasp of pain, but before he could fire again he was seized from behind by someone who had come up noiselessly on the other side of the car and, taking advantage of the door, which had been burst open in the crash, had crept in upon him.

146

He struggled vigorously, but his efforts were of no avail, for the man behind him had thrust a handkerchief, sweet and sickly with chloroform, across his mouth and nostrils.

Holding his breath, the inspector tried to turn his gun upon his assailant, but at the same moment the other door of the car was wrenched open, and his gun was knocked from his hand, while the anæsthetic slowly did its work.

All David's efforts to pull himself together and throw off the fumes were impossible. His efforts at resistance grew weaker and weaker, and he sank into oblivion, his last conscious thought one of fury at himself for falling into the trap so neatly laid for him.

When he came to himself he was lying in an uncomfortable heap on the bottom of a jolting car. He felt sick and dizzy, and as the events of the past hour or so returned to him his exasperation became unbearable.

Escape was out of the question. At first he could not understand what had happened to him, but gradually the realization of his plight was borne in upon him. An old and musty-smelling sack had been forced over his head and drawn down until it held his arms as close to his sides as if he had been wearing a straitjacket.

His wrists were roped to his thighs and his ankles bound.

David felt bitterly angry. He could hardly breathe, and the smell of the sack was intolerable.

He listened intently. He could feel that there were other people in the back of the car besides himself, but no one spoke, and he had no way of telling how many there were.

As far as he could tell, he was riding in a six-cylinder car which was travelling at a fair pace. Accompanying it were two motorcycles. He could hear the throb of their powerful engines on either side of his own vehicle.

At first his heart rose at the hope that they might belong to members of the Mobile Police, who had somehow got on his track, but after a time he abandoned this idea. It had evidently been a considerable crowd who had set upon him, and the motorcyclists were, no doubt, merely members of the gang for whom there had been no room in the car.

He stirred, and instantly a heavy boot caught him in the ribs so savagely that a grunt of pain escaped him. Still no one spoke. The silence of that long, flying journey was uncanny, and David was disquieted. He had no means of protecting himself, no means of helping Judy. There was nothing for it but to wait and see what would happen.

Lying there, he wondered if this was to be the end of everything: this ignominious finish, with his head in a sack.

On second thoughts he was inclined to think that if they intended to kill him they would have done it then and there and would not have troubled to cart him about the country in this silent, grim fashion.

His wrists and legs were numbed by the tightness of his bonds. The air inside the sack was foetid and stifling. He felt himself slipping into unconsciousness again, and it was while he was fighting this new attack that the car came to a sudden standstill.

David heard the motorcycle engines stop also. Then he felt himself seized roughly by the shoulders and dragged out onto grass.

Still there was no sound from any of his captors. Once he thought he heard a man swear under his breath, but the sound was cut off instantly, as though someone had laid a hand over his mouth.

In spite of himself David approved. There were brains in this business, if nothing else. If ever he got out of this predicament alive he knew that he would not have anything, any impression, any half memory, to help him recognize his captors if ever he met them again.

The fresh air slowly filtering through the matted fibres of the sack revived him a little, but he lay limp, although every sense was alert, and waited.

He thought he detected a muttered conference going on some

distance away from him, but although he listened earnestly he could catch no separate word.

Presently the muttering ceased. Once again he was seized by the shoulders, and this time someone else took his feet. There was a stumbling journey of perhaps fifty or sixty yards, and then he was thrown down on the hard earth, his head coming in violent contact with a wooden wall.

Stirring his feet cautiously, he detected another strip of wall and realized that he was lying in a corner of some building.

He waited anxiously for the next move. All about him was ominously quiet. He thought he heard softly moving footsteps going away from him. Then all was silent, until suddenly, from some little distance off, came the sound of a petrol engine.

He recognized it as that of the car in which he had come. He heard her start up and drive slowly off. Listening intently, he heard first one motorcycle and then the other follow her.

The sound of the three engines grew fainter and fainter. Finally they died away altogether.

David stirred. He struggled and tried to sit up. But there was no movement around him, and it was borne in upon him that he was alone.

He spoke, and the sound of his own voice was terrifying in the stillness. He tried to shout, but only the muffled echoes of his own voice answered him.

How long he stayed there he never knew. He felt it must be several hours. Suddenly, far away in the distance he heard a motorcycle engine. He summoned all his strength and shouted. The engine came nearer, and he paused, a cry stifled on his lips. It was either the same machine or one exactly like the first of the two machines which had accompanied his captors.

A thrill of fear went through him. It was something more than physical alarm. There was something positively uncanny and terrifying in the thought of that one lonely rider coming back through the night towards the helpless man who lay bound and stricken in the darkness.

The engine stopped. David strained his ears for footsteps but heard none. And then at his very side there was a movement.

An exclamation escaped him, but he mastered the impulse to cry out.

The next moment the bonds which bound his legs were cut through. Then his wrists were freed. A knife cut through the sacking, and a rush of sweet, clean air came to his nostrils as the ragged hessian dropped to the ground.

"Stand up," said a husky voice. "Put your hands above your head."

David had no choice but to obey. He was far too sick and weak to risk a fight at this stage in the proceedings. His wrists and ankles were tingling unbearably as the blood rushed back to them, and the newcomer pressed a gun into his ribs.

He found he was in a barn. It was only just beginning to get light, and the corner in which he stood was still well in the shadow.

"Walk straight on till I tell you to stop," said the voice at his side.

David made out a lank figure in dungarees, the lower part of whose face was completely covered by a white handkerchief, and whose broad flat cap was pulled down well over his forehead and eyes.

With his hands above his head and the stranger's gun in his ribs David marched out into a lonely country road. A powerful motorcycle stood just outside a farm gate. There was not a soul in sight, nor any signs of human habitation. The barn itself appeared to be ruinous and disused.

"Get on the bike," the newcomer commanded. "I'm coming with you. Try and get away from me and I'll shoot."

The grim determination in the tone convinced David that this was no idle threat. He did as he was told, and two minutes later found himself wobbling unsteadily along a dusty flint road, with his captor, like some old man of the sea, perched on the pillion behind him.

For the first few miles David obeyed instructions implicitly. He knew his only chance was to put the stranger off his guard and at the same time conserve his own strength.

It was still very early, just after five, he guessed. The country was unfamiliar to him, and the road a lonely track along what appeared to be salt marshes and poorly cultivated farm land.

Suddenly David saw his chance. They were nearing a little humpbacked bridge, much steeper than usual. Just before they reached it he put on a spurt and took it at speed.

The jolt very nearly unseated him, and he thought for a second that he had lost his passenger, but he was unprepared for the tenacity of the man. Two extremely powerful arms seized him round the waist, the bike wobbled off the road, and David and his captor came off together.

"That's right, young man," said a voice behind him as he struggled to his feet. "It was about time you and I had a bit of a talk."

David swung round. The clear light of dawn fell upon his captor's face, from which the handkerchief had disappeared.

David stared, too surprised even to speak. Standing in front of him, a little dishevelled from his fall but otherwise very much the same as he had looked on their first meeting, was none other than the odd seafaring person whom he had last met coming out of Judy's room in the Hotel Arcadian in the company of ex-Sergeant Bloomer.

For some seconds David stood quite still, trying vainly to collect his scattered wits. The whole thing was incredible, a nightmare situation in which the very last eventuality seemed to arise.

Who this remarkable old man was, whether he were friend or foe, or what he could possibly have to do with Bloomer, were all questions which raced through David's mind. But a new problem soon claimed all his attention.

The shock of surprise had loosened his iron hold upon himself, that hold which alone had made him capable of overcoming his weakness sufficiently to master the motorcycle. The violent fall to the ground had not helped matters, and now he found to his horror that the world was going black about him.

The fields and hedges, which had been growing momentarily more and more distinct as the dawn advanced, now became blurred again as they seemed to rush past him in an endless stream. He strove vigorously to pull himself together, using every ounce of strength he possessed to combat the deadly nausea and inertia which threatened to overcome him.

But there is no physique in the world which is capable of throwing off the after effects of so powerful an anæsthetic, and he reeled.

The strange old man ran forward to seize his arm, but David saw the earth rise up to meet him and the next moment lay face downward on the thick, dew-soaked grass at the side of the road.

"Where is Judy? Where is Judy Wellington?"

The words, uttered with an impassioned eagerness, came to him through the mists. At first they seemed to him to be the echoes of his own brain, but gradually he became aware that it was not mere fancy.

He was aware of two fierce grey eyes peering into his own and discovered that he was lying upon his back on the grass and that his erstwhile captor and rescuer was bending over him.

"Where is Judy?"

There was no mistaking the urgency of the question.

"Where is she? You know. You must know."

David closed his lips tightly, and as though he understood the reason for the young man's silence the older man went on.

"I'm her friend, I tell you, and I must know. Where is she? Where is Judy? She's in danger, and I've got to find her. You've got to help me find her. The name of the town! What's the name of the town?"

Had David not been temporarily bereft of his critical faculties he could hardly have failed to realize that the man was telling the truth, but for David the world had ceased to exist for the time being. He remembered Judy, Judy in danger. He must get to her.

And then the awful darkness descended upon him once more, and he was gliding along in space at a tremendous rate with no power of guiding himself and no power of turning back.

His next impression was that he was being lifted up none too gently and laid upon something hard which rolled and swayed beneath him. There was a noise too, a familiar mechanical noise, a violent rattling and rumbling which was oddly soothing.

He closed his eyes.

When he opened them again he discovered that he lay on a pile of sacks in the back of a lorry. He sat up. His head was splitting, but the weakness had disappeared. He shivered. The day had broken, and the early morning sun was already gilding the tops of the hedges.

He looked about him. The old man had disappeared.

He shouted to the driver, and when a red, astonished face appeared at the little window in the back of the cab, he beckoned to the man to stop. David swung himself to the ground. He still felt shaky, but no longer giddy, and although his head hurt intolerably his brain was clear.

Standing in the road, he looked up at the sleepy driver and plied him with excited questions. The driver yawned.

"I don't know, mate," he said. "I was stopped about ten miles back by your friend, who explained that you and he had come off your bike going over a humpback bridge. The bike was running all right, and your friend's gone on ahead to prepare some friends of yours at Laidwich and to get them to get ready for you. He seemed to think you were more hurt than you are. What happened to you? Knock your head up a bit as you came off?"

"Something like that," David admitted cautiously as he climbed up beside the driver. "I'll give you ten bob if you get me there before the first train," he said.

"Oh, that's all right. Your friend who took on the bike saw to me. How long had you been lying there? All night?"

"No. Not quite so bad as that," said David, and although the man looked at him inquisitively he did not explain further.

As the lorry continued its leisurely way David went through his pockets, and a savage exclamation escaped him. His money, letters, keys were all quite intact, but the little notebook in which he had scribbled down the list of towns which he had deciphered from the blotting paper in Marguerite Ferney's room had disappeared.

"What's the matter? Lorst something?" said the lorry driver. "Per'aps your friend picked it up."

A grim smile passed over David's lips.

"Perhaps he did," he said.

But the name of the last town on that list was clearly imprinted on his mind. It was Hintlesham. Hintlesham. He must get there without delay.

On arriving at the pleasant market town of Laidwich he pressed a small sum of money on the inquisitive lorry driver and bore down upon the post office to telephone.

David had not forgotten that he was on duty, and however pressing his own private business might be he knew that his first act must be to get in touch with Inspector Winn.

It took him some time to get through to the Westbourne headquarters, and when at last he did so it did not improve his temper to be told that Inspector Winn was away on important business connected with the case, that he had left no message for Inspector Blest, and, although the sergeant did not say so, it was perfectly obvious that Inspector Blest's services were not required by Inspector Winn.

This unexpected and somewhat ungracious release from his responsibilities was extremely welcome, and David made his way to the railway station, a single name beating over and over again in his brain.

Hintlesham!

Judy was in danger, and as far as he knew he might quite easily have put yet another of her enemies upon her track.

15

A MORNING CALL

S HE'S STILL ASLEEP."

Marguerite Ferney stepped softly into the big, luxuri-
ously furnished sitting room and closed the door very gently
behind her, as though even at that distance the slight sound might
wake the girl whom she had left.

The woman herself looked little rested, with the bright
morning sun pouring full upon her face. She was pale, and there
were shadows under her eyes. Although a brave and unscrupulous
woman, she was still feminine enough to be a little afraid of the
man in front of her.

There was something terrifying about his coldness and the
calm ruthlessness of his manner.

Carlton Webb frowned as he glanced up at her and his quick
eyes took in the signs of fatigue and alarm which marred her
beauty. Her pallor seemed to annoy him. He shook his head at her.

"You're letting this thing get you down," he said. "It's very silly
of you. There's nothing to worry about. In the first place, no one
knows where we are, and in the second place, even if they did,
who have we got to be afraid of? Two grossly conceited pompous

old swindlers who are already frightened to death by the enormity of the stupid little crime they have committed."

Before the reproof in his tone Marguerite Ferney pulled herself together. She walked over to the table, and taking a cigarette out of the box, sank down in a chair and waited for him to proffer her a match. But in spite of her languid expression her hand trembled a little as she held the cigarette.

"You think you're very clever, Carlton," she said. "And so you are, my dear, as a rule. But it's not very clever to underestimate one's opponent. That's one of the most elementary of tactical errors, isn't it?"

Carlton Webb laughed and seated himself on the arm of her chair.

"D'you know, I rather like you in this mood, Marguerite," he said. "A little touch of alarm seems to soften you."

"I'm not alarmed." In spite of herself the woman spoke petulantly. "I'm simply cautious. I stand to lose more than you do. My position is more precarious. Tell me, what have you done to that girl?"

Webb laughed. "How does she look?"

"I tell you she's asleep still."

He nodded. "I expected that. But how does she look?"

Marguerite Ferney's big eyes rested upon his face.

"She's very pale," she said, "and breathing a little more heavily than I should have expected. Carlton, you haven't poisoned her? She isn't going to die there?" Her voice rose hysterically.

The man rose to his feet.

"My dear girl," he said angrily, "you're impossible this morning. She's perfectly all right. I shall go up and see her in a moment. You can trust me, can't you? I'm not a complete fool."

The woman turned her head away from him and shuddered.

"You must forgive me," she said, "but my nerves are on edge. Last night when we unlocked the door and found her lying there on the floor completely unconscious I had a presentiment of terror, a sense of failure—I can't explain it."

"Your nerves have gone to pieces," said Carlton Webb, raising his eyebrows and eyeing her with a mixture of annoyance and disgust.

Marguerite went on speaking.

"And then when we lifted her onto the bed and made that injection in her arm I had a feeling of panic. I've never felt like it before."

The man took her by the shoulders and jerked her to her feet.

"Now, look here," he said roughly, "pull yourself together. I tell you everything's going perfectly. The little fool has played into our hands. It couldn't have fallen out better if we'd arranged it for years. Consider the situation: At least a dozen people, including those whom we have most cause to fear, believe that girl to be a permanent invalid. They believe she has no strength or stamina, and nothing could suit our purpose better. Given such a card, if we can't play a decent hand we're imbeciles."

Marguerite shuddered. "What did you do to her? Why does she look so pale? Why does she breathe so heavily?"

"She used to have to produce that pallor by artificial means," said Carlton Webb. "Now that won't be necessary. She used to have to assume a certain weakness. Now that won't be necessary either. I feel my early medical training is coming into use at last. I won't bother you with a lot of details, my dear, but there are at least three drugs in the pharmacopoeia which will produce that effect at least for a short space of time without greatly injuring the patient. So far we are absolutely safe. But I should like to see her when she wakes. She may remember something of what happened last night, and I must prepare her mind. Perhaps this afternoon she will be well enough to see a doctor."

"To see a doctor?" Marguerite sprang to her feet. "Are you crazy?"

"Not at all. I'm perfectly sane. I've never behaved in a more logical fashion in all my life. I'm sorry you're taking it like this. Personally I'm finding it remarkably interesting. It's a situation which amuses me."

Marguerite walked up and down the long room. It stretched the whole length of the house and was on the first floor, so that she could look down into the garden from one window and on to the narrow shrubbery-lined drive from the other.

The man had seated himself again and seemed engrossed in some huge inward joke.

"Here we are, completely hidden," he said. "They can't find us for several days yet, and by that time we shall be ready for them. The legal side of the business may take some little time, but that needn't worry us. Our credit will be high. No one's going to refuse credit to the heiress of a fortune of that size. And then we shall leave this rather depressing country and go, I think, to France. How does that attract you? Paris is very pleasant at this time of year."

The woman did not answer, and he turned upon her testily.

"What's the matter with you?"

A low shuddering cry, half stifled in her throat, escaped Marguerite.

Webb leapt to his feet.

"What is it?"

She was standing by the front window, staring down into the drive, her cheeks ashen and her eyes dilated.

"It's he," she said. "He's found us. He's come."

The man rose swiftly to his feet, and, striding across the room, looked down into the drive himself.

A long low car had turned slowly in at the gates and now stood drawn up before the front door. Even as they stared, a tall thin sinister figure stepped out of it and advanced towards the porch.

"Who is that?" Carlton Webb's voice was unnaturally harsh.

Marguerite shivered.

"That's Saxon Marsh," she said. "He's come. What shall we do now?"

Webb caught her wrist.

"You go and lie down," he said. "Go to your own room and stay there and leave this to me."

Marguerite Ferney shook her head.

"No. I'm all right. Now that something's happening I feel I can pull myself together. It was the waiting and not knowing that unnerved me. Let me stay. It'll look better if I do."

There was no gainsaying this line of argument, and the man hesitated. A change certainly had come over the woman. She looked herself again. There was even some colour in her cheeks.

The old flicker of admiration crept into his eyes as he saw her. She was undeniably beautiful, and there was a poise and self-assurance about her which had not seemed possible before.

She lit another cigarette, and as the two stood waiting, the sound of a quiet precise voice came to them from the landing without. There was a discreet tap on the door and a manservant entered.

"A Mr. Saxon Marsh to see you, madam."

This announcement, which might very well have thrown Marguerite completely off her balance two or three minutes before, had now completely lost its potency.

"Oh yes," she said. "Please show him in, will you, Jones?"

Saxon Marsh entered. He looked very much the same as at their first interview on the little ledge overlooking the sea front when the stone urn of scarlet geraniums had glowed and burned above her head.

He was still dressed in his neat grey alpaca suit, but there was a smile of satisfaction on his thin lips, and his small eyes shone dangerously.

As he entered his eyes were fixed upon the woman, so that Webb had every opportunity of sizing up his opponent.

Marguerite Ferney rose to the occasion magnificently. She rose and went forward, her hand outstretched.

"Dear Mr. Marsh," she said. "How nice of you to come and see me."

But if Saxon Marsh was at all put out by this display of friendliness he did not show it. He ignored the proffered hand and looked steadily at the man, who had risen and stood behind Marguerite. As yet he had said nothing, but his unspoken question filled the room.

"This is my cousin Carlton Webb," she said. "He has charge of my affairs and knows all my secrets."

"Quite a responsibility," said Marsh dryly.

Marguerite Ferney did not appear to have heard.

"Won't you sit down?" she said.

"No, thank you. I prefer to stand. I've come on a very serious business."

The thin dry voice was cold but still quiet.

"I'm here on behalf of my friend Sir Leo Thyn, whose affairs I have taken over temporarily because of his indisposition. Miss Ferney, I'm afraid I must ask you to deliver up his ward immediately."

Marguerite Ferney and Carlton Webb exchanged glances. Then the woman laughed.

"My dear Mr. Marsh," she said, "aren't you taking rather a preposterous attitude? My little friend Judy Wellington fled to me for protection, and I shall certainly do all I can to assist her in every way."

Saxon Marsh smiled. "Very pretty," he said. "But somehow I don't see you as a philanthropist, Miss Ferney."

Marguerite rose to her feet with great dignity. In her cool morning gown, with her silver-blonde hair drawn down to a neat knot at the nape of her neck, she made a queenly and imposing figure.

"My dear," she said, turning to Webb, "I think you had better see to this business for me."

She walked stiffly out of the room, leaving the two men alone. Webb lounged forward.

"My dear sir," he said in that easy, nonchalant way which he knew so well how to affect, "you're behaving rather absurdly, don't you think?"

Saxon Marsh eyed the man quizzically. He was not altogether taken in by that lazy smile, and the careless, rather foolish expression which the other man had assumed did not deceive him for a moment.

"If I am to believe that you are Marguerite Ferney's adviser," he said, "don't you think it would be well to warn her that the police of this country are not lenient in cases of abduction?"

"Here, I say, you know, that's a bit thick," said Webb, still maintaining the character he had assumed. "There's also a law of slander, I believe. You'll have to be very careful what you say."

"Judy Wellington is in this house," said Saxon Marsh. "It is my duty to take her back to her guardian, and I intend to fulfil that duty."

"Miss Wellington is not very well at the moment." The words were drawled, but the narrow eyes were fixed upon the other man's face for any trace of emotion it might show. "Her nerves are completely upset. She fled to my cousin for shelter and is now receiving every care and attention. Before you come here making ridiculous demands I should advise you to consider what authority you have. If Sir Leo Thyn is so anxious about his ward, why doesn't he come and fetch her himself?"

"I have told you that Sir Leo is not well," said Saxon Marsh patiently. "I have come to take the girl to him. I should like to see her, please."

"I'm afraid that is not possible." Webb was speaking with the cold deliberation of one who realizes that the advantage is all upon his side. "I'm afraid I can't help you."

He advanced towards the door with the obvious intention of holding it open for his unwelcome visitor.

Saxon Marsh sat down.

"Mr. Webb," he said, "you and I should understand one another."

Webb turned back halfway across the room, his eyebrows raised. For a moment neither man spoke as two pairs of eyes took stock of one another: the one so pale and expressionless, the other so bright and narrow. Neither flinched, and Saxon Marsh's tone became more conciliatory.

"Has it occurred to you, my dear Mr. Webb," he said easily, "that you and your—er—cousin are playing a very dangerous game? Oh, don't misunderstand me. I'm not for a moment suggesting that we should enter into each other's confidence. But I think it is to our mutual advantage that we should each see where we ourselves stand. Think it over, my dear sir. Is the game quite worth the candle?"

Carlton Webb laughed softly, and, ignoring the other man's question, said easily:

"I'm very glad to have met you, Mr. Marsh, but I'm sorry your visit has not been productive in any other way."

Marsh did not seem to hear the flippant compliment. He leant back in his chair and folded his long thin hands.

"Miss Wellington is a charming girl," he said, "though hardly the friend I should have chosen for your—er—cousin. However, quite apart from her personality, she has another more material qualification to recommend her to Miss Ferney's attention. I don't think I need explain to you what that is."

He glanced sharply at the other man, but Webb showed no sign of any emotion save something which might possibly have been boredom.

Saxon Marsh went on softly and precisely.

"I am interested to hear that you are showing some concern for Miss Wellington's health. But perhaps I ought to tell you that she is not quite the invalid which she appears. That is a fact known both to me and to many other people who know her well."

He paused, and Webb cut in.

"I'm afraid all this doesn't interest me very much," he said. "My cousin is very fond of Miss Wellington and is looking after her in every possible way."

"How kind of her." Saxon Marsh spoke gravely. There was not the faintest tinge of sarcasm in his voice. "How excessively kind," he continued. "But perhaps I ought to warn you of one thing. Consider your responsibility. Miss Wellington is ill. You have admitted it yourself. Suppose she should die. There would be a very thorough investigation, and, since your cousin has something to gain by her death—though not a lot, Mr. Webb; let me repeat, not a lot; not quite so much, perhaps, as she imagines—then it might be very awkward for you both."

Webb laughed. "You can rest assured, Mr. Marsh," he said, "that whatever happens to Miss Wellington will stand the most thorough investigation."

There was a strange smile on his lips as he spoke, and Saxon Marsh, looking up, saw the smile and understood. He rose slowly to his feet.

"You will hear from me in the very near future," he said. "But meantime I imagine I can take back to Sir Leo the full assurance that Miss Wellington is being looked after."

Pausing before the window, he added with apparent irrelevance:

"This house has a very lonely situation."

"Yes," said Webb grimly. "We have a large staff."

Saxon Marsh still laughed, but there was a grim expression behind his eyes. He had not expected to find this sort of opposition. In the doorway he paused.

"I consider your action most discourteous and reprehensible," he said. "The next time I come to see you it will be to bring Miss Wellington away."

Webb smiled slowly and enigmatically.

"We shall be ready for you," he said.

As Saxon Marsh drove slowly down the drive of that strange gaunt house, two people stood at the sitting-room window and watched his departing car. When it was out of sight Marguerite Ferney caught her companion's arm.

"You got rid of him?" she said huskily. "There's something terrible about him, something dangerous. Didn't you feel it?"

The man ignored her.

"Is the girl awake?" he demanded abruptly.

"I don't know. I haven't been in. What are you going to do?"

"Keep your nerve," he whispered. "Keep your nerve."

Marguerite swallowed noisily.

"He'll come back," she said in a strange hoarse voice utterly unlike her own.

The man nodded grimly. "Oh yes, he'll come back. He didn't come here with any hopes of getting the girl. D'you know why he came, my dear Marguerite? He came to spy out the land."

"And that means—?" The woman was white and trembling.

Carlton Webb dropped a kiss upon her forehead and, taking her chin in his hand, looked down into her face.

"That means we've got to hurry," he said. His voice sank upon the last word, and the air in the bright room seemed to have become strangely cold.

16

THE MEN IN DISGUISE

NO, SIR. I'm sorry, sir. No room at all."
The landlord of the White Lion, the one hotel which the tiny township of Hintlesham possessed, spoke with a certain amount of satisfaction, a fact which David found oddly irritating in the circumstances.

"Booked right up, we are," the man continued, and added gracelessly that he was not a one for company.

David, tired and exhausted with his journey, and still shaken by the tumultuous events of the preceding night, turned away from the oaken bar and stood for some moments looking out of the small lattice window at the cobbled square.

He had only just left the railway station and had been hoping to find someone from whom he could learn something about the district.

The landlord had proved singularly surly, however, and he was waiting patiently for the next customer when he was surprised to see a long grey car which looked oddly familiar pull up outside the inn.

Almost immediately a hand seized his arm and a familiar voice said huskily:

"This way, Captain. You don't want to let 'im see yer."

David swung round and stared into the pink and happy face of ex-Sergeant Bloomer, late of the Metropolitan Police.

Bloomer, in disgraceful flannel trousers and a sporting jacket, was an even more unprepossessing figure than Bloomer collarless and in carpet slippers. But this was Bloomer triumphant. This was Bloomer while the going was good.

He laid a finger on his lips, and, taking the inspector's arm, led him up to the bar, where they were not visible from the open doorway to the passage.

He was only just in time. There was a clatter of feet outside, and David heard a voice which he recognized at once. It was not a voice that one easily forgot.

"Marsh," he said.

"That's right. 'E's staying 'ere. 'Im and a whole gang of toughs. Nice old gent, isn't 'e? Not up to any good, either. 'E's the one to be careful of, if you ask me. Now, come on quick," he added as the last footstep died away. "Me and my friend have got the little back room on the second floor. We can talk there."

David suffered himself to be led up the narrow, roughly carpeted stairs. The little room into which Bloomer showed him was a bedroom, with clean covers and a low raftered ceiling.

Bloomer seated himself upon the bed and regarded David solemnly.

"I'm sorry I 'ad to drag you away like that," he said. "But if you'd been seen it might 'ave given the game away."

David turned upon him.

"Look here, Bloomer, what's all this about?" he demanded. "What are you doing here, anyway?"

"Pursuin' my own investigation and givin' a friend a hand," said Mr. Bloomer, who seemed to have lost entirely his hangdog expression, and whose lugubriousness was obviously entirely a thing of the past. "And if you'll forgive me sayin' so, Captain, I've got a fancy that you and me are on the same track. So why shouldn't we join forces? We're both after the same young lady, aren't we? Miss Judy Wellington. Well, per'aps if you're not *au fait* with the situation, Captain, as they say among the Frogs, I may as well let you know that she's in a house not far from 'ere, and Mr. Marsh 'as just come back from an interview with the lady who's keepin' her a prisoner. You know this is better than old times, isn't it? Better than anything I've come across before."

David was silent. This was an entirely new aspect of the case. He regarded Bloomer thoughtfully.

The ex-sergeant, he knew, must be interested solely in the murder of Johnny Deane, and if, as he supposed, Judy's father was still the suspect, then Bloomer could only be anxious to get hold of the girl in his attempt to find her father.

However, the main thing was to find Judy and bring her to safety. He had been convinced that Sir Leo had not been lying in that outburst at the Arcadian. That sort of admission he knew from experience was nearly always the truth.

He opened his mouth to speak but changed his mind. Bloomer had risen from the bed and had hurried over towards the door. There were footsteps on the stairs outside.

Bloomer opened the door cautiously.

"All right," he said huskily. "Steady on there, mate. We've got a visitor."

A man came hurrying into the room and stopped impulsively on the threshold, an exclamation on his lips.

David too had risen from his chair by the window. The man facing him was Bloomer's companion of his visit to the Arcadian, the man who had rescued and then attacked him only a few hours before. He was begrimed with oil and dust, and he looked gaunter and more disreputable than ever.

It was David who spoke first.

"There'll have to be an explanation," he said quietly.

The man sank down on the edge of the bed where Bloomer

had been sitting. For a moment he remained passive, his head bowed. Then he looked up and seemed to pull himself together with a tremendous effort.

He was old, David noticed again, old in spite of all his strength and spareness.

"Explanations can come later," he said. "You shall hear everything. But not now. Now we've got to save her. She's in that house. Those fiends have got hold of her. Good heavens, man, don't you realize she's in danger? Real danger! Even Marsh couldn't get any satisfaction from those people. I saw it in his eyes as I waited in the hedge for him to come out."

"You don't think he noticed you?" It was Bloomer who cut in, his small eyes sharp with interest.

"Oh no. I kept well behind them. Besides, the roads aren't so very lonely. There's plenty of other motor-bikes. I stopped when I saw him turn in on the drive, and went on on foot, keeping behind a hedge. I tell you I saw his face as he came out, although it was only for a second as the car flashed by me. He looked like a disappointed fiend. I'm going to get in touch with the others. If they're going to attempt some rescue by force we may be able to use them for our own ends and get her away. We couldn't do it on our own. It would be fatal to attempt it. It might only hurry them in their project on her."

His voice rose unsteadily.

"There are eight men there. We couldn't do it alone, you and I, Bloomer. But perhaps with this young man——" He looked at David dubiously and broke off.

Bloomer shook his head and glanced at David. But that young man was staring at the newcomer, an odd expression in his eyes. There had been something in the agony hidden in the voice which had awakened his memory, and now, rising to his feet, he strode across the room and peered down into the old man's face.

Even that most effective disguise in the world, the simple

change of class and type with but the faintest of artificial aids, cannot bear so close a scrutiny.

There was a moment of dead silence. Then David straightened his back. Although he had only seen the man once before in his normal appearance, he recognized him now.

A wave of comprehension passed over him, but a comprehension not untinged with amazement when he considered Bloomer's part in the deception.

"You are Lionel Birch!"

The man rose to his feet and, turning away abruptly, went over to the washstand, where he effected several minor but startling changes in his appearance. Then he turned round.

"Inspector Blest," he said, "I am Jim Wellington. Judy is my daughter. Will you sit down? I should like to have a few words with you."

For a long moment there was silence in the room. This was an eventuality of which David had never dreamed, and his first reaction was one of intense astonishment at the part Bloomer must have played in Lionel Birch's extraordinary escape. But always at the back of his mind was the urgent fear for Judy and the passionate desire to get her in safe hands as soon as possible.

He sat down at last and faced the other man, his eyes questioning.

"I think Sergeant Bloomer here told you that he recognized me when I first entered the Empress Hotel," Birch said, speaking in a strange detached voice, as though his emotions were fixed on something quite different, as indeed they were. "Twenty years ago I held a very good position in a firm of solicitors. One day there was a crash. A burglary had been effected, and it was proved by the police that the evidence had been largely faked and that the job had been done from the inside. Unfortunately a policeman had also been attacked.

"I won't bother you with details of my trial, and I won't weary you by assuring you that, just as the evidence of the burglary had been counterfeited, just so was the evidence against me. Unfortunately, the second time the real criminal got away with his deception. I was sentenced and served my time in Dartmoor."

He paused and looked at David earnestly. The boy found it impossible to suspect the sincerity of that quiet voice and the honesty of those cold, pain-stricken eyes.

"Yes," he said softly. "Go on."

"When I came out of Dartmoor," continued the man who had once been Jim Wellington, "the first thing I did, not unnaturally, was to change my name. I became Lionel Birch. From then on my life was very difficult. I should have gone abroad, of course, had it not been for one thing. My wife, whom I adored, had died while I was in prison, but our daughter Judy was alive, and I wanted to be near her. Therefore I went to her guardian, Sir Leo Thyn."

As the name left his lips a very curious expression passed over his face, and David began to realize some of the hatred which the man before him had felt for that much-respected figure.

"He had a very good reason for helping me," Lionel Birch continued grimly. "He had been junior partner in the firm from which I had been so ignominiously dismissed, and although of course I had no proof, I was sure as anyone may be sure in this world that it was his crime for which I had paid the penalty, his crime which had cost me my wife and my liberty and my career."

His voice shook. David could see that he was in the grip of a tremendous nervous strain. All the hatred and resentment of the past twenty years was evident for a moment in his voice.

"Well," he said at last, "he did help me. He was the child's guardian and the administrator of the fortune which a relation of her mother's had left for her. While the child was young he was content that I should have her. We lived in a little cottage on the Suffolk coast, and I suppose I was as happy as I ever had been since the few brief months of my marriage.

"I taught Judy to read. I brought her up, and I trained her mind. But as soon as she was fourteen or fifteen Sir Leo wanted to take her away from me. Neither she nor I could bear the parting, although she knew me only as her uncle. It was then we hit on the deception of which you have heard. As far as Sir Leo was concerned, she became a chronic invalid. I had a friend, the local doctor, now unhappily dead, who helped me with my deception. I told him as much of the story as I dared, and I think he guessed the rest.

"Sir Leo understood that Judy could not leave the district without grave danger to her health, and as he was particularly anxious that she should live to inherit her fortune, he let her stay."

He paused and sighed.

"The rest I think you know. The time came when for his own ends it was necessary that she should marry. For my sake, she kept up the deception. I was so frantic about her that I followed her to Westbourne, and, staying at a different hotel, made an arrangement to meet her every evening.

"It was after the first of these meetings that I returned to the Empress to find I had taken her case. It was that case which you returned for me, Inspector."

David nodded. Delicate ground had been reached. He knew that his duty required him to take a statement, to warn the man that anything he said might be used in evidence against him, but for some reason he did none of these things, but sat quiet, listening. There was something compelling about the man, a quiet dignity combined with a passionate intensity of feeling which was quite irresistible and convincing.

"Judy had told me that she had been introduced to the man Sir Leo intended her to marry. I tried to get her to describe him, but she could not. She seemed hardly to have noticed him. She could not even remember his name. She seemed to me to be thinking of someone else."

He looked at David sharply, and the young man felt his heart move uncomfortably in his side.

"You can believe me or not, Inspector," Birch continued, "but I did not know at that time, nor at the time of his death, that Major Deane, who had a room on the same floor as myself, was the man whom Sir Leo had picked out to be the husband of my girl. Had I known as much about him as I do now," he continued, "believe me, I might easily have been moved to murder, but my victim would not have been the insignificant little swindler who was merely carrying out one of his more despicable projects for the sake of a few pounds. I should have killed the man who had conceived the abominable idea, the man who was prepared to sacrifice my daughter, just as he had sacrificed me, for the sake of his own worthless hide. And if you're a man as well as a police-man, Inspector, I think you'll agree with me that I should have had good cause."

David said nothing. His official capacity made him necessarily dumb. But he could not help sympathizing entirely with that pale, tortured man who stood before him.

There was silence again in the low hotel bedroom. It was broken rather surprisingly by Bloomer, who had sat quiet in a corner during the old man's story and now heaved himself to his feet and came forward with a slightly self-conscious swagger.

"P'r'aps while we're 'aving this little talk I ought to explain where I come in," he said. "I don't want you to get me wrong, Captain, and I'd like to point out that I'm a free agent, as it were. Not connected with the police any longer."

David began to understand. Bloomer's red face wore a slightly anxious expression which would have been comic at any less crit-ical moment, and it occurred to David that he was doing his best to make a confession which at the same time would reflect a certain amount of glory upon his own perspicacity.

"You may remember, Captain," he said, clearing his throat, "that I had a few words with Inspector Winn on the night the murder was discovered. Well, I went off almost in a 'uff, as you might say."

He paused, and his small eyes sought David's questioningly, as though imploring for a certain amount of decent human tolerance.

"I don't mind confessing," he went on, "that I was a bit above meself, what with one thing and another; a bit—how shall I say?"—he waved his plump hands—"well, anxious to get me own back."

David conquered a desire to smile. The spectacle of Bloomer boiling under the affront to his dignity returned to him vividly.

"So you went upstairs and arrested Inspector Winn's prisoner yourself?" he suggested.

"Well, no, I didn't exac'ly do that." Bloomer was beginning to look uncomfortable. "I just moved 'im into another room, and we 'ad a bit of a chat. I understood 'is point of view, and 'e understood my intentions—why, even a child, Captain, could see 'e's not the man the inspector wants! Anyone can see that 'e's telling the truth. After all, consider it, Captain, why should 'e go and kill a feller that's going to marry 'is daughter when 'e knows that as soon as that chap's out of the way the old bloke with the title was goin' to dig up someone else? It's not reasonable, is it? Think, Captain, think. . . ."

David sighed. He was beginning to understand the extraordinary state in which Lionel Birch's room had been left on the night of the murder. It had been systematically untidied by someone without much imagination, and that someone, he saw now, was none other than ex-Sergeant Bloomer.

"I put 'im in me own room for the night and rigged 'im up," Bloomer continued modestly. "In the morning it was the easiest thing in the world for me to get 'im out of the 'otel and bring 'im back again as an old friend of mine. Everybody was so busy looking for the murderer, they never thought of suspecting my old friend.

"As a matter of fact," he continued with justifiable pride, "the disguise was very good. It took you in and everybody else."

"Why on earth did you go to see Judy?" The Christian name escaped David in spite of himself.

"Oh, we had to. Just to let 'er know 'er uncle Jim was all right. We told 'er not to worry and she'd 'ear from us soon.

"I must admit," he continued, blinking thoughtfully at David, "*you* gave me a bit of a shock, sir. But I carried it off all right, didn't I?"

This last remark was too much for David. He smiled. The ex-sergeant's tremendous satisfaction was too much for his gravity.

"Bloomer, this is disgraceful," he said.

The old man laughed. "I know. I wonder at it meself sometimes. But, after all, you can 'ave too much of officialdom. You've got to follow your own inclinations sometimes. Well, there you are. I've done it. I admit it. Now then, Captain, you know everything. What are you going to do?"

David was silent for some moments. His duty was very clear.

"I ought," he said at last, "to arrest you both and take you to Westbourne."

Bloomer rose and moved quietly to the door.

"Somehow I don't think you're going to do that, Captain," he said.

David sprang to his feet, but Lionel Birch stood in his way.

"I'll answer for Bloomer," he said, "and for myself too. We must get Judy to safety. Once I know she is in safe hands I give you my word I will accompany you to face any charges you may care to bring against me. I saved your life this morning, Inspector. I had instructions from the leader of the gang of ruffians who stopped you last night to drag you out of the barn when the others were safely out of the way and throw you into one of the dykes in the saltings, which are covered with water at high tide. As soon as the water had gone down, your bonds were to be removed and your body would have been found drowned with no explanation."

He paused and went on again quickly:

"Since my 'disappearance' I have been playing the part of a down-and-out willing to do anything for a few shillings, and in that capacity I was able to join the select company with which Mr. Saxon Marsh, Sir Leo's associate and, I should say, master had seen fit to surround himself.

"Help me to save my daughter."

David sat very still. He knew what he intended to do might easily cost him his position, won so hardly in the past few years. But he also knew that nothing really mattered to him in the world except Judy, and now her father's appeal was answerable in only one way.

"We'll get her," he said. "In the ordinary way it should be possible to enlist the authorities on our side, but in the circumstances I don't see quite how we can do that. After all, she went away with Miss Ferney of her own free will."

"Poor Judy!" Lionel Birch spoke softly. "She didn't know. I didn't warn her. How could I? The last time I saw her I did not even know myself. Marguerite Ferney, you see, is the other heir. If Judy dies, Marguerite inherits the fortune."

David was aghast. "She wouldn't dare, in that case," he said. "She wouldn't dare to do Judy any harm, unless—"

He paused, not caring to finish the sentence.

Lionel Birch nodded. "Exactly," he said grimly. "Unless she was certain she was safe. I wish Silas Gillimot's fortune was at the bottom of the sea rather than that it should bring Judy so much danger."

David sighed. "I wish to God it were," he said, and the bitterness of his tone told Lionel Birch something which he had been wondering for some time.

He sighed with relief. Inspector David Blest was no fortune hunter.

The older man plunged into his scheme with alacrity.

"It's a big lonely house on the coast, and closely guarded," he said, "but I think we three might attempt it if we waited until dusk. The other person we have to contend with is Saxon Marsh himself. He's more dangerous than the other two, although Webb is an unknown quantity as far as I'm concerned."

David opened his mouth to speak, but the words were silenced by the sound of a departure in the yard below their window. He sprang to the casement and, peering out, was just in time to see Saxon Marsh step into his car, which shot out into the road at an alarming speed.

Almost immediately two or three men, who were quite obviously part of the bodyguard, entered a second car which thundered after the first.

The whole departure was made with such terrific haste that David was puzzled.

"It almost looked like a flight," he said aloud. "I wonder what new monkey business this is."

He was answered by Bloomer, who had just come into the room, a newspaper in his hand. His face was flushed with excitement.

"He's gone," he said. "Paid 'is bill and skedaddled like a rabbit. Now we're going to see the feathers fly! And if you ask me, Captain, I think I can explain that little exit.

"The evening papers have just arrived," he continued, "and very enlightening they are, too. Take a look at the front page, will you, Captain?"

David took the proffered news sheet and read the paragraph which Bloomer indicated so triumphantly.

The Welbourne Police [he read in the small type beneath the flaring headlines] *this morning interviewed Sir Leo Thyn in a nursing home in Harwich. Late last night Sir Leo was interviewed by the police before embarking upon the Flushing boat. It was after this interview that Sir Leo became unwell and was taken to a nursing home in the town. It is understood that the baronet was too ill for a long interview this morning, but it is believed that Inspector Winn, of the Westbourne County*

Constabulary, is remaining in the town in the hope of a further inter-
view this evening.

"There you are!" Bloomer's voice was triumphant. "Sir Leo's
lost 'is nerve and 'is old friend Saxon Marsh is going to help 'im
out. And if you ask me," he continued with an elaborate wink at
the inspector, "'e's goin to see 'is old friend doesn't open 'is mouth
too wide."

17

THE WITNESS IN THE CASE

DEFINITELY NOT MORE than half an hour, Inspector, and I grant that only against my better judgment. Sir Leo is in danger of a complete collapse. I warn you, his reason may be permanently impaired if he is subjected to any worry at this stage."

Like a great many other members of the unenlightened public, the doctor felt that the police were going a little far in their persistence in worrying so eminent a man as Sir Leo Thyn, especially when the affair which they were engaged in investigating could, everybody felt, have nothing to do with the distinguished lawyer.

Inspector Winn knew himself to be at a disadvantage, but never had his determination stood him in better stead. He clung to his task with an obstinacy which in the circumstances did him credit. Neither snubs nor downright rudeness put him off his self-appointed task.

It was true that he was investigating the death of an unworthy person, and the witness who had first put him on to the baronet would make an even more unattractive figure in the box than the deceased Johnny Deane might have done, but Inspector Winn felt he was nearing the truth, and the more he saw of Sir Leo the more convinced he was that Nifty Martin had been right.

Inspector Winn had not much experience of people of Sir Leo's type and class, and the man's reputation and title impressed him in spite of himself. But the fact remained that Sir Leo was behaving exactly like any other badly frightened man Inspector Winn had seen, and were it not for the fact that the whole thing seemed so extraordinarily unlikely, the inspector would have sworn that Sir Leo was a guilty man.

However, he nodded gravely to the doctor.

"I quite understand, sir," he said in his most conciliatory manner. "I understand perfectly, and you can rely on me to see that the unfortunate gentleman is not disturbed any more than is absolutely necessary. But I have a witness here whom I am very anxious Sir Leo should see, and if you don't mind I'll take her in."

The doctor glanced past the inspector to the shabby little figure who sat nervously in a corner of the big waiting room playing with a pair of dingy cotton gloves. Ruth Dartle was not at her best when she was nervous, and at the moment she was more or less paralytic with embarrassment. Inspector Winn almost felt he ought to apologize for her presence in that soberly magnificent building.

The doctor sighed.

"Very well. If you must, I suppose you must."

He went out, and Inspector Winn turned to the girl. He had rehearsed her a dozen times but was never sure whether she had understood what he was saying or not.

"Now, don't forget," he said kindly, for he found that any severity in his tone reduced her to a state of complete blankness of mind. "When the nurse takes us in I want you to move round and look the gentleman full in the face. When he speaks I want you to listen to his voice. If you recognize it you can nod to me. If you don't, keep quiet and follow the nurse out of the room and come back here. Understand?"

"Yes," said Ruth dubiously, and inwardly Inspector Winn groaned. Every witness in this case, he reflected gloomily, seemed either to be completely unpresentable or a congenital idiot.

These gloomy thoughts were interrupted by the arrival of a somewhat supercilious young person in nurse's uniform. She conducted the ill-assorted couple down a narrow parquet-floored corridor to the far end of the building. Then, with a gesture enjoining quiet, she ushered them through a white enamelled door into a sun parlour, one of the private wards kept for convalescent patients.

It was a pretty little room, very bright and tasteful, one wall of which had been entirely replaced by special glass through which there was an uninterrupted view of a charming flower garden.

Sir Leo, a mere shadow of his former self, was sitting huddled in a big wicker chair, his head supported by a great bank of down-filled cushions. He sat up stiffly, however, when he caught sight of the inspector, and his face wore an expression of ludicrous terror.

Inspector Winn glanced sharply at his companion. The girl was goggling at the man in the chair, but there was no sign of recognition on her face, and when she caught the inspector's eye she shook her head. When the nurse went out the girl followed her, and a great wave of depression passed over Inspector Winn.

Sir Leo remained in his uncomfortable upright position. Gone was all the ease of which he had been such a master.

"What do you want?" he said in a thin high voice utterly unlike his own. "I tell you I am ill—ill. You've got no business to come bothering me. Who was that woman? Why did she stare at me? I tell you I've nothing to say—nothing to say at all."

Inspector Winn coughed depreciatingly. Behind his little sharp eyes his mind was working rapidly. The man was in a state of abject terror: he could see that. Why, his lips were blue and his pupils contracted. And yet he was not guilty—or at least, the girl had failed to recognize him.

Inspector Winn wondered savagely whether the girl was

capable of recognizing anybody or remembering anything. He gripped his notebook and cleared his throat.

"Sir Leo," he said gently, "this morning, if you remember, just before you were taken with your fainting fit, you told me that you had never heard of a man called Johnny Deane, alias the Major. Then, if you remember, you changed your mind and said that you thought you had heard of him but believed it was some time ago. I have here a note written by you to Mr. Deane on the morning of the day on which he died. Could you perhaps give me an explanation of the discrepancy in the two facts?"

It went against the inspector's grain to treat a man who was so evidently lying with such gentleness and deference, but he was still more than a little impressed by the other's eminence, and the girl's reaction had taken a great deal of the wind out of his sails.

As his last word died away the other man hunched himself up in his chair and spoke again, still in the high, unnatural voice which told of a cracking nervous system.

"I tell you I don't know. And I won't be questioned. D'you hear me? I'm too ill to be questioned. You can't question a sick man, probably a dying man. Didn't the doctor tell you, you might drive me mad? He ought to have told you that."

"But, Sir Leo, I must have an answer." In spite of his care a touch of authority had crept into Winn's tone.

To his delight, the other man reacted to it. The unaccustomed severity seemed to pull him together, and it was as though, the inspector reflected, a pail of water had been poured over a hysterical girl. He noticed with delight signs of returning normality. Sir Leo's brain was beginning to work again, and he was becoming cautious. He put his hand up to his forehead.

"Let me think," he said. "I'm sorry, Inspector, but my brain seems to have gone completely. I must have had some sort of stroke."

He laughed, and the sound was meant to be apologetic. It

sounded unnatural even to himself, however, and he became grave again.

"Let me think," he continued. "Mr. Mazarine, you say? No, Inspector, the name is unfamiliar."

Winn blinked. The man must be well at the end of his tether if he was going to attempt puerile subterfuge of this sort.

"No, Sir Leo," he said. "You know very well that I've been talking about a man called Johnny Deane, who called himself the Major. You wrote a note asking him to come and see you at the Arcadian Hotel, Westbourne. That note is now in my possession."

A smile of understanding which was only too obviously assumed passed over Sir Leo's face.

"*Deane?*" he said. "But how absurd of me! Of course. It had quite slipped my memory. He was an unfortunate down-and-out sort of person, Inspector, who approached me in London with a long story of his hardships. I am inclined to be a sentimental old fool where ex-service men are concerned, and I told him that I was going away on holiday and would need a chauffeur for the trip. He came to see me at the Arcadian, I remember. Not a very satisfactory person. I didn't engage him."

He paused, and the expression on his face was terrible inasmuch as there was a forced smile of bland politeness on the lips, while the eyes were wild and terrified.

Inspector Winn was shocked. He got a glimpse of the man Sir Leo had been in the days of his greatness, in the days before he had lost his nerve, and it was somehow shocking to see him transformed into an unconvincing shadow of his former self.

Inspector Winn looked down at his notebook.

"I have here a deposition from Charles Wade, a waiter at the Arcadian. In it he states that you treated the man Deane as a friend, introduced him to your ward, and finally took him up to your suite. Do you always engage your chauffeurs that way, Sir Leo?"

"Do I understand that you don't believe me?" Sir Leo meant

the question to be dignified. Instead it sounded like an entreaty. He lay back and closed his eyes. "I can't answer you any more," he said. "I can't say anything. I'm ill, I tell you, ill! I—"

His voice cracked.

Inspector Winn rose to his feet, but before he could reach the door it was opened, and a nurse and the doctor reappeared, and with them a man whom the inspector did not recognize.

Saxon Marsh was at his most imposing. Never had the tremendous personal force of the man been more apparent. There was an air of authority and dignity in his very bearing.

He glanced at Inspector Winn as at an entirely unworthy object.

"It is a damnable thing," he said, and his voice was none the less impressive by virtue of its very quietness. "Here is a famous man, an important man, on the verge of a nervous breakdown of the first magnitude, and a pack of interfering noisy policemen are let loose upon him and permitted to ask him banal questions, aggravating his condition. I'll speak to the commissioners myself, doctor. Don't worry."

The two men and the nurse looked coldly at the inspector, and it was the doctor who spoke.

"If you have quite finished, Inspector Winn, I should be glad if you would let my patient have a little rest. I'm afraid your visit has only done him a lot of harm. I hope it has been more satisfactory from your point of view."

Inspector Winn squared his shoulders. It was on occasions such as this that his tenacity was best displayed. The snub passed over him like water over a duck's back.

"I shall have to see Sir Leo again," he said.

"My dear sir, talk about that later." The doctor spoke testily. "If you don't leave him alone you'll see him in his coffin."

He had lowered his voice so that the man in the chair might not hear, but Saxon Marsh appeared to be very shocked by the possibility of their being overheard and ushered the little group out into the corridor.

"This is my card," he said, thrusting a slip of pasteboard into the inspector's hand. "You'll hear of me again. And now, if you'll excuse me, I'll go and see my poor sick friend."

Accompanied by the nurse, now even more supercilious and disdainful than before, the unfortunate inspector made his way back to the waiting room to collect his unsatisfactory witness.

Here a delay occurred. Inspector Winn, boiling with indignation and very uncertain in his mind as to the correct course for him to adopt, decided to make a bold stand.

"I think I shall wait here until I hear when Sir Leo can see me again," he said.

The nurse stared at him, her eyes widening.

"Really!" she said.

But the inspector was not to be put out by a little chit of a girl.

"That'll do from you, miss," he said meaningly. "You run along and tell the doctor I'm going to wait."

With her cheeks flaming, the nurse strode out of the room and came as near to banging the door as nurses ever do.

There was a long silence, which was broken by Ruth.

"I'd never seen the little fat man before," she said. "It wouldn't do for me to say I had if I hadn't, would it?"

"Oh, good heavens, no," said the inspector savagely. "Don't get ideas like that in your head. Tell the whole truth and nothing but the truth."

Once again there was a pause, which again was broken by the girl.

"Didn't he look ill?" she said. "I thought he was going to faint, didn't you?"

The inspector made some inaudible reply, and Miss Dartle, finding him in no mood for conversation, relapsed into injured silence. At last, in exasperation, she got up and walked over to the window, where she stood looking out onto the formal strip of garden in front of the imposing building.

Inspector Winn remained immersed in his own gloomy thoughts. He saw himself getting into trouble through no fault of his own, and the prospect was hardly comforting.

So engrossed was he that he did not hear the soft footsteps in the hall without, nor did he notice the murmur of discreetly subdued voices, and it was only a shrill scream from the girl at the window which brought him to the present again.

"Look!" Ruth was pointing in front of her. "Look! There he is. I'd know 'im anywhere. That's 'im. I'd swear it! Whatever they do to me I swear it. It's 'im. Look!"

The inspector was by her side in a moment.

The man whose card was in his pocket, the man who had introduced himself as Saxon Marsh and whose name he thought he vaguely recognized, had just come out of the building and was standing talking outside his huge grey limousine to the doctor who had accompanied him.

Ruth lifted a pale, excited face to the policeman.

"That's the man who was in fancy dress. That's the man who told me he was Lionel Birch and asked the way to Major Deane's room. . . . Swear it? Of course I swear it! Who's goin' to forget a face like that in a hurry?"

The girl's voice died away, and there was silence in the waiting room before the inspector decided to make a move. Miss Dartle was, he felt sure, the sort of witness of whom a clever King's Counsel would make a most distressing exhibition in any witness box, although she certainly seemed convinced enough at the moment.

It was unfortunate that all these things should have had to pass through Inspector Winn's mind at such a critical juncture. However, the law of the land being what it is, he could hardly rush out on the spot and make an arrest.

This consideration did not occur to Ruth Dartle, however. Her pale stupid face grew suddenly pink with anger, and she showed a spirit with which Winn would not have credited her.

"Well, look," she said, "there he is! There's the man. There's the man you're looking for. Why are you waiting? Don't let him get away!"

In her extreme excitement her voice had become shrill and penetrating, so penetrating, indeed, that even the heavy glass of the window could not quite stifle it. It reached the ears of the man outside.

Saxon Marsh turned abruptly, and for an instant his eyes rested upon the scene in the window: the excited, gesticulating girl, and behind her the inspector in uniform.

Instantly Winn's doubts of Ruth's testimony were dispelled. He saw the expression on the skull-like face of the man outside, saw the quick shadow of alarm pass over that cadaverous countenance, and the next instant Marsh had shaken hands with the doctor and, leaping into his car, had shouted a word of command to his chauffeur which was instantly obeyed.

The doctor's jaw dropped. He was evidently astounded that the conversation should have ended so hurriedly.

"He's gorn!" Miss Dartle was loud in her disappointment. "You've lorst 'im! I thought you policemen were so quick on the uptake. You've let 'im get away. That's the man, I tell you. I'd swear it—I'd swear it anywhere, on me dying oath."

She was becoming hysterical again, and Inspector Winn caught her wrist.

"You be quiet," he said firmly. "You've done your part, and you've done it very well, and I shall need you later. But just at the moment, for God's sake, hold your tongue."

"Well, I must say—" began Miss Dartle, but, catching sight of the suppressed excitement in his eyes, she shut her mouth abruptly and watched him with eagerness.

Inspector Winn drew the visiting card which Saxon Marsh had given him from his waistcoat pocket. He felt the surface with a sensitive thumb. Both name and address were engraved, and the inspector sighed. The chances were against its being a fake.

He read the address very carefully. Then, taking Ruth firmly by the arm, he piloted her straight out of the building and across the street to the nearest call box.

Ruth had to wait outside for quite a long time while the inspector was talking, but when he came out she noticed that he seemed extraordinarily pleased, and even went so far as to buy her a packet of chocolate as a reward for her assistance.

18

THE TWO WHO HURRIED

M Y DEAR, how long you've slept. How do you feel?"
Marguerite sat on the end of Judy's bed, looking cool
and inexplicably lovely in a long, shadowy blue gown which
seemed to enhance the fairness of her hair.

Webb stood behind her, his hands in his pockets, his habitual
good-natured expression on his face, entirely convincing had it
not been for a certain eagerness in his narrow eyes.

Judy lay in bed and stared at the ceiling.

"I can't understand it," she said. "I feel completely exhausted.
It's awfully late, isn't it?"

"After lunch," said Marguerite, smiling at her. Now that the
woman had something to do, all her previous nervousness had
vanished, and she looked calm and completely natural.

Judy was puzzled. "It's very queer," she said. "Very queer
indeed. I've never felt like this in all my life before. How terrible
of me, Marguerite, to come to your house and get ill immediately.
It's almost like a—a—" she smiled ruefully—"a judgment on me
for pretending, isn't it?"

"Oh, my dear, you're not ill. Don't worry." Marguerite was

gently reassuring. "That's why I've brought Carlton in. He used to be a doctor, and I thought he might have a look at you."

Carlton Webb wandered over to the bed and took the girl's hand. He held the limp wrist thoughtfully in his own for a moment or so, and then, bending down, felt her forehead and peered into her eyes.

"Good heavens, no," he said. "You're all right. It's just a collapse brought on by nervous excitement. Nothing to get worried about. Just take things easy for a bit."

Judy hesitated. She could not tell why it was that she disliked Carlton Webb. She only knew that she did dislike him very intensely. There was something odd about him, something slightly conceited and insincere, yet not definite enough for her to feel sure that she had not imagined the whole thing.

Marguerite patted her hand.

"Don't worry, my dear. I know what that sort of shock is. I was completely exhausted myself after that wretched accident at the hotel. You looked after me then, and I'll look after you now. You're not in any pain, are you? Is there anything I can do?"

"Oh no, I'm not in pain." Judy frowned. "I'm perfectly all right really—only terribly weak. And—I know it sounds absurd to say so—I had the conviction that I was drugged last night. That last cup of tea, it tasted awfully queer, and I think I fainted after it. Oh, I know," she went on quickly as she caught a glimpse of the care-fully simulated shocked expression on the other woman's face, "I know it's quite the craziest mistake. I just wondered if something could have got into it by accident or something. I remember trying to get over to the door and finding it locked."

"Locked?" Marguerite raised her eyebrows. "Judy darling, you are light-headed."

Carlton Webb smiled ruefully. "It's rather hard on us to say things like that, Miss Wellington," he said. "After all, we're doing our best to make you comfortable and—"

"Oh, I know." Judy was profoundly unhappy. "Don't misunderstand me. I'm only telling you about the ridiculous experience I had. I know it must have been all a dream now, but it seemed so real then that I thought I ought to let you know. I suppose," she went on lamely, feeling that her apology was going down badly, "I suppose this wretched business must have been coming on then. I hope it's not a sort of flu."

"Good heavens, no. You can take it from me that it's just a natural reaction after overexcitement." Carlton Webb spoke convincingly.

Judy frowned. Her face was very pale, and, like all naturally healthy young people when suddenly overtaken by illness, she was secretly afraid of her own weakness. It seemed so extraordinary.

"In a way—" Marguerite looked up at her cousin with what appeared to be a faintly mischievous expression upon her lips— "this indisposition of Judy's may be a blessing in disguise. In view of our visitor this morning, I mean."

Carlton Webb took his cue.

"Well, yes. I hardly like to mention that in view of our young friend's headache. However, perhaps I ought to."

Judy tried to sit up in bed. "What is it? Something about my uncle?"

"No, my dear, no. You'll hear from him soon." Marguerite's tone was soothing. "But we had a visit from Saxon Marsh this morning. Do you remember him? A friend of your guardian."

Judy lay very still. Things that had been terrifying enough when she was completely fit and mistress of herself had now become unspeakably horrible when she was weak and exhausted.

"What did he want?" She hardly recognized her own voice.

"You." Marguerite grimaced as she spoke, as though there were nothing at all frightening in her statement.

"Don't let him take me—please! Oh, please, Marguerite!"

"Of course not, of course not. Carlton, this child is very nervy still." The woman patted the slender little hand lying on the coverlet. "But he's a rather importunate person, and it wasn't easy to get rid of him."

"You did send him away, then?" Judy sighed with relief.

Again Marguerite glanced at the man behind her, and Judy read in her face only the polite question which was whether the patient could safely be told some triflingly exciting piece of news.

Webb answered the unspoken inquiry.

"Well, yes," he said. "I think we might tell Miss Wellington. After all, she's got to know some time or other, hasn't she?"

"Oh, what is it?" Judy's lips were quivering.

Marguerite put out a protective hand.

"My dear child, don't worry. It's nothing alarming. You see, I told Mr. Marsh that you were not at all well; much too ill to receive visitors, in fact. After all, it was a half truth, and he was such an odious person that I was sure you would want to get rid of him."

Judy nodded, but her eyes were still anxious.

"And then what?"

"Well, then, my dear, he went, but not very graciously. In fact, I'm afraid he indicated pretty clearly that he did not believe I was telling the truth. What he proposes to do is to send a doctor to see you this afternoon.

"Now, don't be alarmed," she went on hurriedly, as the girl caught her breath. "I should get up, if I were you. Go and sit in the garden. I'll have some deck chairs put out there, and you can look cool and interesting and pale in the shadow of the trees."

Carlton Webb, who had been watching the girl, his narrow eyes taking in every change of expression on her pale face, interposed.

"I'm afraid you've got to face it, Miss Wellington," he said. "This man Marsh, and I presume Sir Leo too, seem to suspect the bona-fides of the illness you have so cleverly counterfeited. I presume you don't want them to find out the truth, do you?"

"Oh no, of course not—of course not." Judy looked horrified.

"But what shall I do? He'll discover me at once. Oh, can't you prevent him from seeing me?"

Again Marguerite glanced at the man, and this time there was an ill-concealed smile on her scarlet lips, a smile, however, which Judy was too overwrought to notice.

It was Webb who spoke.

"Now, look here, Miss Wellington," he said, coming forward, "you know your own business best, and I hesitate to suggest any deliberate deception unless you feel it really necessary, but if you are convinced that it is vital for your guardian not to know of your own and your uncle's subterfuge, then let me suggest something. You're not well this morning, and any doctor hastily examining you might be forgiven if he mistook your symptoms, which are purely nervous, for something more serious. However, he will only do that if you tell him the same story that you have told all the other people who have been to see you so far.

"After all," he went on, speaking persuasively and gently as though to a child, "doctors are not magicians, you know. At best they're only clever detectives. They add the evidence which you tell them to the evidence of their own eyes and draw their verdict from the two."

"That's right, Judy." Marguerite spoke soothingly. "And I shall be with you the whole time. I'll steer him away from any difficult questions. You just stick to your original story, and you'll see that you'll come through all right. And this evening I expect your uncle will attempt to make some communication with you."

Judy nodded. She was still wide-eyed and frightened.

Marguerite sighed. A very difficult interview was at an end.

"I'll send someone to help you dress, dear," she continued. "Don't try and brace yourself for the ordeal this afternoon. Remember you've only got to convince a rather foolish old doctor that you're not well. I shouldn't think that'd be at all difficult. You look terribly pale."

Judy watched the two go out of the room. Although the day

was warm she was cold, and her limbs were trembling. The dreadful lassitude which had come over her in the last few hours could not be shaken off. She felt ill, much more ill than ever in her life before.

In the passage outside the door Marguerite Ferney looked up at Carlton Webb.

"All right?" she whispered.

Carlton Webb nodded. "Yes," he said, and added under his breath, "So far so good."

19

MURDER PLOT

I T'S SO TERRIBLY AWKWARD for me, doctor. I don't know Miss Wellington very well. To be quite frank, I only met her a few days ago at the Arcadian Hotel at Westbourne."

Marguerite Ferney was at her most charming. In a soft grey cotton dress with a white ruffle at the neck and sleeves she looked very demure, very young, and very feminine, and Dr. Doe, the busy general practitioner for the district, glanced at her with approval. He was interested in this tall, fair woman who had rented the house for six months in the summer and who kept such an enormous staff of servants.

He was a plump, pompous, conventional little man who had naturally had no suspicions aroused by his telephone summons to the household. Visitors often called him in for trivial ills, and this sort of call came naturally in his day's work.

Marguerite went on. "Of course, she's a permanent invalid. She told me so when we first met, and it seemed so sad that one so young should be staying all alone in a big hotel that I took pity on her and brought her home with me for a week. I'm afraid the journey didn't do her any good. She looked so terribly pale and worn this morning that I felt I really must have a doctor just for my own protection. She assures me that it's nothing at all unusual, but I thought I would like a medical opinion. I do hope you don't think me very foolish."

She looked archly at her visitor on the last word, and Dr. Doe replied gallantly.

"Most natural, my dear lady, most natural. Let me have a look at the young lady."

Marguerite noted the placid expression upon his face and smiled to herself. She was an adept at handling this type of man, and she knew quite well that the opinion which had been formed in his mind was just the one she had attempted to create.

They walked through the house towards the garden where Judy was sitting under the trees. She looked like a little ghost. The vivid scarlet of the garden cushions enhanced the deadly pallor of her face and lips.

The doctor stepped forward, and, after shaking hands, began in his best bedside manner.

"Well, young lady," he said. "A bit under the weather? What's the trouble?"

Judy's eyes flickered. This plump, amiable little person was very different from the imposing London specialist whom she had imagined her guardian, Sir Leo, might send.

"I'm just a little tired and weak, doctor," she began hesitantly, trying to keep her eyes away from Marguerite's face.

The doctor noticed this tendency and applied an entirely erroneous explanation to it. He took Judy's wrist, felt her pulse, and, as these told him very little save that the girl was obviously in a state of great weakness, asked the obvious question.

"Now, tell me, how long has this been going on?"

Judy did not meet his eyes. "My guardian knows quite well," she said, "that I've been ill since I was thirteen. I assure you I'm very little worse than I always am. I've told Miss Ferney that I only need two or three days' rest."

Her voice was very faint, and her habit of avoiding Marguerite

Ferney's glance convinced the doctor that she was ashamed of having planted herself in the house of a woman who did not know her very well and then having to confess that she was always very delicate.

"You have your own medical man at home, I suppose?"

"Oh yes, of course."

"And you don't feel very much worse now than you usually do?"

"No." Judy spoke hesitantly. "I'm a little nervy, I suppose. I don't want to see people or travel,"

"I see." Dr. Doe smiled. "Well, I'm inclined to agree with your own diagnosis, young lady. Take it easy and you'll soon get back to your normal state. I'll send you down a bottle of medicine, something to make you sleep."

To Judy's complete astonishment he rose, and, after shaking hands, made his way across the lawn with Marguerite strolling gracefully at his side.

Judy was bewildered. It had been a most unexpected interview, quite different from the stern catechism she had both expected and dreaded. This man was just like some nice little country doctor who realized that she was only a visitor and would not be long a patient of his own, rather than a man Sir Leo had sent to wrest the truth from her and force Marguerite to give her up.

She saw Miss Ferney and the little doctor in earnest conversation as they reentered the house and wondered what they were saying. Had she been able to hear, her bewilderment might well have increased.

Marguerite was playing her part very well.

"Then you don't think I need worry, doctor? That's such a weight off my mind. I was so afraid I might have to bundle her off to hospital or something. As you say, it's not wise to invite home people one doesn't know very well."

Dr. Doe looked at her slyly.

"Oh, no fear of that, dear lady," he said. "You may have to put up with her for a day or two, and then I should send her back where she came from. I didn't go into her trouble very fully because she evidently has her own medical man. You can see she's an invalid. Her pulse was weak and that pallor is very pronounced. But if she's properly taken care of she may last for years. I don't know what her trouble is—pernicious anæmia or something of that sort. She evidently seems to regard it as quite the normal thing."

Marguerite Ferney saw him to the door. She was very charming, very graceful in her thanks, and Dr. Doe bustled off on his long round convinced that he had met a very charming woman who, through her own kindness of heart, had been temporarily saddled with an invalid.

As soon as his busy little car had shot out of the drive, Marguerite Ferney ran up the broad staircase and tapped at the library door. A minute or so later she was seated on the arm of Carlton Webb's chair, talking excitedly.

"He swallowed it like a lamb," she said, "and the girl played up magnificently, without realizing it, of course. She still thinks he was sent by her guardian, and he's positively convinced that she's just the invalid everyone thought she was at the Arcadian. How's that?"

"Splendid, my dear Marguerite, splendid. So far it's gone through perfectly. But we're not out of the wood yet. This is the beginning."

Carlton Webb's voice was very grave.

"We mustn't make a false step anywhere. However, at the moment everything's perfect. That man's evidence will be most useful at the inquest."

Marguerite shuddered. "I hate to hear you use that word," she said. "She looks very ill. Very ill indeed. I almost believe my own story. You haven't done anything . . . that can be traced?"

"Nothing at all. I've told you, Marguerite. I'm not a fool. In a couple of days, if she's left entirely as she is, that girl will be as fit and well as ever she was. She's just weak now. That's all. It's rather as though she's been starved. However, we've accomplished the first two steps. Now we must take the third. We must establish our alibi, that's the important thing. We've got to be somewhere else, somewhere where we can be seen at the very moment that our young friend meets with her unfortunate accident."

He rose to his feet and, linking his arm through the woman's, stood for a moment staring through the broad window, across the lawn to the dazzling strip of water beyond.

"It looks very peaceful, doesn't it?" he said, and added with a little laugh which had in it something so completely callous that Marguerite shivered. "No one would dream of those currents. Quite the most dangerous on the East Coast, aren't they? Even on a day such as this."

Marguerite turned away. "You frighten me, Carlton," she said huskily.

His grip on her arm startled her with its force.

"Don't be a fool. It's nearly over now."

They found Judy lying back among her cushions. She looked up anxiously as they approached.

"That funny little doctor, he didn't guess, did he?"

"No, my dear. He's gone off with a most satisfactory report from our point of view for Sir Leo. He says you're to take it very easy for at least three days, so you're safe for that time, at any rate. And meanwhile your uncle will have arrived. I can't think what is delaying him so long."

A shadow of alarm passed over the girl's face, and Marguerite went on.

"Never mind, my dear. You're quite safe with me."

Judy looked up at her gratefully.

"You're incredibly kind, Marguerite. I'm afraid I'm being an awful nuisance."

Carlton Webb smiled. "Of course you're not," he said. "By the way, Miss Wellington, Marguerite doesn't want me to ask you this, but I feel I ought to. After all, it's only a few hours, and I know you won't mind. You see, it's Marguerite's birthday today, and on these occasions she always takes the servants over to Loo, which is miles away on the other side of the bay, to a local fair and concert. It's over about ten o'clock, and I know it wouldn't amuse you. But I wondered if you'd mind if we didn't alter our plans. You'd be perfectly safe here alone, you see, and we shan't be very late. The arrangement has been made for some time, and I hate to disappoint the servants."

"But of course not."

Webb smiled at the eagerness with which the girl rose to the bait.

"Of course not," she repeated. "I shall be delighted. I can sit here until I feel tired, and then I'll go to bed."

Marguerite shook her head. "I can't have it," she said. "I can't have you left here alone. It seems so rude."

She paused, anxious lest she had made her protest too strong.

"Of course not," said Judy. "I'd like to be left alone—really I would."

Carlton Webb clinched the matter.

"Oh, well, then," he said, "that simplifies everything. I'm so glad we shan't have to disappoint the staff after all."

Judy lay back among the cushions and closed her eyes. She felt too weak even to be frightened.

Carlton Webb nodded secretly to Marguerite, and together they moved softly and exultantly away.

Marguerite came across the lawn to say goodbye to her just after five o'clock. She looked very lovely, Judy thought, her long silk coat and picture hat a fitting accompaniment to her befrilled gown of ninon.

"Now, my dear," she said, "you're sure you'll be all right? I feel a complete pig leaving you alone, but I don't like to disappoint the staff. Your room has been prepared for the night, and you'll find all the refreshment you want in the dining room. I've had a cold meal laid out there. We shall lock all the doors and windows at the front of the house, so you'll be perfectly all right here, won't you? We shall be back about half-past ten. Good-bye, dear."

She stooped as though she were about to kiss the girl, but thought better of it. It was as though some shadow had passed between the two women. Judy felt the checked impulse and wondered, but only for a moment. She repeated her statement that she would be perfectly all right, and Marguerite hurried off.

Judy remained looking after her, and as the slender, graceful figure disappeared into the house something made her raise her eyes, and she caught a glimpse of Carlton Webb standing in the library window looking down at her. He disappeared the moment her eyes rested upon him, and she had no time to see the expression upon his face, but an unaccountable thrill ran through her, a feeling of terror she could not in any way account for.

She pulled herself together. It was this terrible lethargy that had come over her, this strange lack of strength which made her feel so helpless and afraid.

It was over an hour later, when the sun had disappeared behind the cliff and the long golden fingers were stretched out across the lawn and the sea beyond, that she heard the telephone bell. It rang insistently, its shrill trilling piercing through the warm sunlight and demanding attention.

Judy pulled herself painfully to her feet. She had only just enough strength to walk, she found, and her head felt light and swimming.

She made her way into the front hall where the instrument stood, and shivered a little. The great place seemed very dark and lonely after the warm brightness of the evening.

She took up the instrument and pressed it to her ear. The first thing she heard was her own name, "Judy Wellington," muttered in the muffled, unrecognizable voice which any cross-country line seems alone able to produce.

"I want to speak to Judy Wellington."

"Yes?" she said. "Who is it? Judy Wellington speaking."

"Oh, is that you, Judy? Thank God! Can you hear me? The line's very bad. It's I—Uncle Jim."

"Oh, my dear, I hardly recognized you!"

Such a wave of relief passed over the girl that any suspicion which might have been aroused by the peculiar indistinctness of the voice was prevented from arising.

"Listen, Judy." The voice, although by no means clear, sounded urgent. "I can't come near the house—the roads are being watched—but I must see you. It's a matter of life and death. I'm going to the disused building on the other side of the bay. I should think you could see it quite distinctly from the lawn of the house."

"Yes, I can." Her voice was shrill with excitement. "A lonely, square place on the other side of the river mouth."

"That's it. I'm going there. As soon as I arrive I'll put a light in one of the upper windows. Now, listen, Judy. I want you to come. Is it possible? Can any of the people there lend you a boat?"

"They're all out," she said. "But, never mind, I'll get there some-how, darling, if I have to swim for it."

In her excitement she forgot her weakness. Her only desire was to get to the man who called her.

"I'll put a light," the voice continued. "Get a boat. There's sure to be one there. Good-bye, my darling."

There was a faint click at the other end of the wire, and then silence. Judy listened intently, but there was no further message. She hung up the receiver and started off towards the garden door.

At the sudden vigorous movement she all but fell again, and with a sense of dismay she realized her terrible physical weakness. But Judy was no coward, and now she was moved by one of the strongest impulses in the world. She had no means of knowing that the message was false, and for her the command was one which had to be obeyed.

Somehow she got through the garden and down to the beach. She had noticed a boathouse there, and now found to her relief that it was unlocked and contained a tiny rowing boat, quite light enough for her to handle alone.

At first she thought she was to be defeated in her efforts to get it launched, but with a thrill of satisfaction she realized that the tide was coming up and that soon it would flow over the sandy bottom of the shed and lift the boat itself.

She walked back to her seat under the trees and sat there watching the square building across the bay. It was just a little square speck, seeming no bigger than a rabbit hutch, and although she strained her eyes she knew that she would never be able to detect any movement round about it.

She even searched the house for some field glasses, but found none, and came back disconsolate.

To her despair, her exhaustion seemed to be growing rather than diminishing, but, working it out in her own mind, she thought she could manage it. After all, the boat was light, and the distance seemed short.

The bay looked completely calm, with only the merest ripple indicating where the waves rose and fell.

Gradually the time passed. The sun sank lower. Judy strained her eyes. Surely there was a light in the upper window? At first she was not sure if it were the rays of the setting sun reflecting on the glass, but as the horizon grew more grey she saw that it was indeed a light.

With stumbling feet she hurried to the boat-house. The little craft was afloat. Completely oblivious of everything but her desire to get to the man to whom she considered herself a daughter, she stepped into the water and guided the boat out into the shallows.

It took her a tremendous effort to climb inside, and each oar felt as though it had been made of lead. But the light still beckoned her, blinking across the grey water.

Judy grasped the oars. It seemed a very long way, and it was going to be a tremendous test of endurance, she knew. What she did not know was that the river, flowing down against the incoming tide, made currents of which even the most experienced fishermen of the East Coast were afraid; currents against which no single man could hope to pull a boat to safety.

Judy took a deep breath, and the next moment she did what Carlton Webb, sitting safely in his stall surrounded by a crowd of witnesses and miles away from the scene of departure, felt sure she would do.

She pushed the little boat out into midstream.

20

THE LAST THROW

THERE'S NOT a light in the whole blinking house."

Bloomer lowered his voice as he spoke.

"It seems a funny thing to me, doesn't it to you, Captain?"

The two men were standing together in the dense shrubbery which surrounded the drive of the great gaunt house. It was just dusk, and the hour at which Lionel Birch had considered it best to attempt the rescue.

Cold fear assailed David, but he did not speak, and it was left to Bloomer to utter the thought which was in both their minds.

"I 'ope we're not too late."

David caught his breath, and his mouth set in a hard, firm line. A soft rustling in the bushes sounded close at hand and Lionel Birch himself moved softly up beside them.

"All doors locked," he murmured. "The place seems to be empty."

It was very eerie standing there in the swiftly growing darkness, the trees overhead soughing gently in the light wind, but none of the three men who stood so grimly in the shadows had time or inclination to notice anything of that sort. Their minds were fixed upon their project, their ears strained to catch the faintest sound which might lead them to the girl they sought.

"We'll get in somehow," said David doggedly. All his old caution had deserted him. He was thinking only of Judy. "There's a wall round the side there. I'll scale it and try one of the garden windows."

"Careful, Captain." Bloomer spoke warningly. "It may be a trap."

David smiled bitterly. "I almost hope it is. I'd like to get my hands on some of these gentry."

They followed him gingerly across the path, their feet scrunching noisily on the gravel. David rediscovered the wall, and, leaping up, caught the parapet and hung there a moment before swinging himself over.

Still all within the house was silent as the grave, and Bloomer, at any rate, was conscious of a growing conviction that the birds had flown.

Once in the garden, with the others close on his heels, a surprise awaited David. The house was open and the French windows onto the lawn swung wide.

They entered the building, their guns drawn, and as they made a tour of inspection a growing sense of bewilderment seized all three. A fire was still burning in the kitchen, cold food was laid out in both the dining room and the servants' hall, and there was every evidence not only that the house had not long been unoccupied but that its residents intended to return.

They located Judy's room and found it empty, but it still contained her clothes. All her hats and coats were still in the wardrobe.

"It almost looks as though they left her here," said David wonderingly. "Unless—" The word died on his lips. He could not bring himself to utter the awful thought which had passed through his mind.

He moved to the window and looked down into the darkening

garden. He could see the dim outline of the lawn and the white froth of the gentle waves on the beach. There was no moon, and the sea beyond looked grey and mysterious.

Suddenly his attention was caught by something, and his smothered exclamation brought the other men to his side.

"Bloomer," he said, "what do you make of that?"

The ex-sergeant followed the direction of his gaze and whistled softly.

"Looks to me like a signal," he said.

David was staring fixedly at the light in the top window of the disused house across the bay.

"That's about it, Captain." Bloomer was trembling with excitement. "I know this place fairly well. I've been 'ere before. As far as I know there's no one living just across the bay there. It's a lonely sort of place. The town's higher up the river. That's what that is. It's a signal. I wonder—"

But David was already out of the room and hurrying down the stairs. They followed him across the lawn and came up to find him flashing his torch into the empty boathouse.

The tide was on the turn, and already the tiny waves were receding, leaving the floor of the shed smooth unbroken sand.

"She's been here. This is Judy's. I bought it for her myself."

By the light of a match Lionel Birch was examining a blue scarf which he had picked up from higher up on the beach. Judy had worn it in the garden and had dropped it in her haste to get to the boathouse.

David cupped his hands and shouted through them.

"Judy! Judy! Judy!"

There was silence, and then his only answer was the far-away cry of a startled sea gull. He tried again, his strong clear voice echoing through the night.

"Judy!"

There was silence for a moment, and then from very far away, and so faint that at first they thought it was a hallucination, there came an answering hail. They listened intently, and it came again, carried to them by the faint breeze from over the water.

"Help me! Help me!"

Lionel Birch shouted like a maniac, and Bloomer, his small blue eyes round with anxiety, whispered in David's ear.

"God knows what's happened, Captain," he murmured. "I know this bay—it's notorious. There's two or three cross-currents that make a reg'lar whirlpool out there. What are you going to do?"

David stripped off his coat.

"I shall have to swim for it," he said. "There's not another boat. You go and phone, Bloomer. Try and get some help. And you, Mr. Birch, see if you can get her to go on calling us. That'll give me a chance to find her. Thank God it's not misty."

Lionel Birch shook his head. "I can't let you take the risk, my boy," he said. "I used to be a first-class swimmer once upon a time."

David shook his head, and his voice was very quiet and compelling in the grey darkness.

"No, I'm sorry," he said. "This is a job for me."

He called the girl again, and again the faint halloo returned. To his anxious ears it sounded weaker now and yet more frantic.

He waded out into the water and struck out in the direction of the sound. David was a fine swimmer. He cut through the water with long powerful strokes. All his weakness of the morning had vanished, and he swam confidently.

At about a hundred yards from the shore, however, he began to realize what Bloomer meant by cross-currents. He entered a belt of icy water flowing much more swiftly than that through which he had come. Its strength surprised him, and as he went on he found himself dragged this way and that and realized that it was all he could do to keep himself on his course, while progress was almost impossible.

From the shore behind him he heard Birch's agonized voice

shouting to the girl, and while still battling with the water he listened anxiously for the reply.

It came at last, still far beyond him and a little to his right.

Having breasted the cold current he came to a patch of warm water, and then into another current, a violently flowing stream which took him some way out of his course, and he had to wait for Judy's shout before he could fight his way back into position again.

At last he saw the boat. His eyes had become accustomed to the light, and it seemed to him that the moving clouds had actually permitted more light to reach the surface of the water.

He made out the tiny craft with great difficulty. It was not moving, or at least it seemed to be drifting only very slowly.

He ploughed on and was well nigh exhausted when at last he stretched out his hand and reached the gunwale.

Judy was crouching in the bottom of the boat. At the sound of his voice a scream escaped her. Then she burst into tears.

David, scrambling into the boat, found her on the point of exhaustion. Both oars had slipped overboard, and she seemed to have not even enough strength to sit up. She clung to him like a child and lay sobbing on his shoulder.

David held her close.

"Don't worry, dear. It's all right now. What's the matter? What happened?"

She sobbed out her story, and David began to understand.

"I haven't any strength," she said. "I kept on rowing, but the current pulled me out of my course. I thought I was going to die. But I got past one stream, and then I think I must have fainted. When I came to myself I heard someone call, and I was alone out here, and the oars had gone. There aren't any rowlocks, you see."

David made the girl comfortable as best he could and then took stock of the situation. He could not hope to get the boat back to shore as it was, and he had the uncomfortable feeling that the craft was drifting more swiftly now. He shouted to the shore, and, although there was an answering hail from Lionel Birch, no words were distinguishable.

However, David did not worry. Bloomer, he had no doubt, had done his telephoning by this time, and a motorboat was being launched to find them.

A few minutes later his alarm increased again, however. The boat was certainly moving more swiftly now. She was being urged along by a force which he knew must be irresistible. Faster went the little boat and faster, and David began to understand what Bloomer had meant when he had said "a reg'lar whirlpool." The water had become choppy, and the little boat was none too safe. At any moment he felt she might overturn. But there was nothing to do but to wait.

Judy lay with her head on his shoulder, her face ashen in the dimness.

Once the little boat dipped and shipped so much water that he was forced to bale feverishly. It was a nightmare situation.

He realized that Judy was ill, and his anxiety for her increased at every moment. The little boat was speeding on, dipping and rolling on her perilous journey. From far off across the bay the light blinked and wavered. It seemed little nearer now that it had been from the shore, and David realized that the journey was much longer, besides being a thousand times more perilous, than he or the girl had dreamed.

And then suddenly, when the darkness seemed to have settled over them again and the water seemed to be licking the sides of the little boat malignantly and hungrily, the thing that David had prayed for happened.

A beam of light swept out over the surface of the water, and at the same time the soft chug-chugging of a motorboat engine reached his ears.

David was surprised. Bloomer had summoned aid much more quickly than he dared hope. But there it was, and he rose in his seat and signalled frantically, while the boat rocked unsteadily beneath him.

The searchlight passed over them and then ran along the coast, picking up the lonely house with its darkened windows. It hovered over the garden, and David strained his eyes to catch a glimpse of either of his companions who might signal the little boat's whereabouts to the rescue party.

To his surprise the motorboat seemed to decide to put in at the end of the garden, and he shouted vigorously, waving his arms to summon assistance.

Suddenly those in the boat seemed to hear. The searchlight was directed full upon them. Judy scrambled up beside the young man and waved also.

David heaved a sigh of relief. The searchlight remained where it was, and he heard the motor-boat turn and speed through the water towards them.

As it bore down upon them the dazzling searchlight completely blinded the young people in the boat. Judy, overcome by the strain, had dropped to her knees.

David braced himself. He realized that the rescue was not going to be effected without a considerable amount of difficulty.

At last the motorboat was upon them, and David saw to his surprise that it was a much more powerful craft than he had suspected. A gruff voice hailed him, and the question which came over the speeding water was unexpected.

"How many of you are there?"

"Two. There's a girl here. She's fainting. Can you take us off?"

There was a muttered consultation aboard, or at least a pause in which one might have taken place, and then the same voice spoke again.

"We'll try and come alongside."

It was a long and ticklish business, but at last it was accomplished. Two brawny arms in a seaman's jersey drew Judy aboard, and David himself followed. He was not assisted, but made a flying leap from his own foundering boat and landed beside the girl.

He bent over her anxiously.

"Judy! Judy dear, are you all right? We're quite safe now. There's nothing to worry about. Don't get alarmed. There's nothing to be afraid of any more."

He heard her sigh and felt her little cold hand seize his own. And then the light of a powerful flash lamp shone suddenly in his face, and the last voice in the world that he expected to hear said softly:

"Inspector David Blest, I believe. Perhaps you will raise your hands above your head. I have you covered with a revolver. I have two assistants aboard, and I assure you that they are not a pair even a man of your physique would be advised to take on single-handed, especially in a boat which carries such precious cargo."

David knelt up stiffly. The blood seemed to have turned to ice in his veins, for he knew quite well, without any further telling, that the man who bent towards him, the gleaming gun barrel catching the light from his torch, was Saxon Marsh, his own and Judy's most dangerous enemy.

21

MY FUTURE WIFE

"SINCE IT IS probably your last voyage in any boat, Inspector, may I hope that you are comfortable?"

By the faint light reflected from the giant beam which picked up their course, David could just see the thin, skull-like face of the man who sat opposite him.

Judy was lying, a little huddled heap, on the seat at the man's side. The two members of the crew were at their duties, one at the wheel and the other at the searchlight.

Their own little boat lay far behind, for, for the past half hour, the motorboat had been headed straight for the open sea.

David was powerless. For Judy's sake, he knew his only chance of saving them both was to keep still and bide his time. Saxon Marsh's heavy revolver was trained directly upon his body, and he knew that at the first movement the man would fire unhesitatingly.

"Perfectly comfortable, Mr. Marsh, thank you," he said. "Even my clothes are drying. If it is not an impertinence, may I inquire where we are going?"

Saxon Marsh smiled. "No impertinence at all. Although you will not accompany us all the way, Inspector, I think at least you are entitled to know something of your own and your young friend's ultimate destination.

"In the first place," he went on, his voice still precise and conversational, "perhaps it would interest you to know that you are going to die. It is only because I prefer travelling with a live man rather than with a corpse, a fastidiousness you may perhaps find surprising in me, that you are not dead already. I prefer to consign your body to the open sea, Inspector. It would suit my purpose better if you were washed up with your skull broken open on some foreign shore."

He paused.

"The foreign police have not quite that passionate interest in the ultimate fate of their English confreres which the Metropolitan Police feel for their immediate colleagues. As I intend to return to England eventually, you will see that I am naturally anxious not to have my peace of mind disturbed by a lot of official questions."

David leant back and watched the man through half-closed eyes. He wondered what kink it was in that cold, calculating brain which made Marsh so anxious to torment his intended victims. The man was enjoying himself, he felt instinctively. There was an irrepressible satisfaction in his voice, a flavour of contentment which he was evidently quite unable to hide, even had he so desired.

David decided to play up to this weakness. It seemed a very slender thread at which to grasp, but at least it was a thread.

"I commend your forethought, Mr. Marsh," he said. "Tell me, do you intend to make your departure from England in your present craft? I suppose she would take you across the Channel?"

"My dear sir—" Saxon Marsh was amused—"I'm not a young man. At my time of life one doesn't go gadding about the world asking for danger. My yacht is waiting for me. In fact," he went on, "she's been waiting for me since six o'clock this evening. But I am on time. My captain will be suitably gratified. I am not always so punctual. Owing to a fortunate chance, and yourself, my dear Inspector, I have been able to accomplish what I set out to do with the minimum of trouble and danger to myself. But of course you don't understand."

"I'm afraid I don't," said David drily. In spite of the iron hold he was keeping upon himself he found that quiet voice uttering this series of villainous disclosures maddening in the extreme.

"Since we still have a little time, perhaps I will explain."

Again there was that satisfied ring in the voice.

"Circumstances have arisen which make it imperative for me to leave the country for some little time. I am afraid I was recognized this morning by a most undesirable young woman, and since she was backed by a singularly efficient-looking police inspector, I thought it as well to disappear for a time. It was then that I communicated with the captain of my yacht.

"However, I was determined not to let go the prize on which I had set my heart. I am a wealthy man, Inspector Blest, and I wish to continue to be a very wealthy man until I die. I decided to pick up my fortune, therefore, on my way out of the country. I hope I am not boring you?"

"Not at all," said David grimly.

Saxon Marsh sighed. "How pleasant it is to have an interested hearer! Really, Inspector, I shall be quite sorry to lose you. Well, then, I had ascertained where my fortune lay, and it occurred to me that, although its stronghold would be very well guarded by land, it was most unlikely that its sea approach would be at all protected. I came down the coast intending to snatch Miss Wellington from the arms of her self-styled protectress and to carry her off in a romantic fashion which I thought might appeal to her youthful heart. I admit the actual kidnapping, for I am afraid it would have been kidnapping, might have given me some little difficulty, but I am glad to say that with your assistance I was able to accomplish it with practically no trouble at all. You, my dear Inspector, are the only unexpected addition to my scheme. I am afraid it will cost you your life, but in the circumstances I don't see how that can be helped."

He was silent, and remained smiling enigmatically, his gun still carefully trained upon the young man.

Judy stirred, but she did not rise, and Saxon Marsh patted her shoulder, although without looking at her, for his eyes were still fixed warily upon his captive.

"Poor little girl," he said. "I am afraid it will take her some time to forget you, Inspector. However, for your comfort I should like to say that I shall do my best to see that she is well treated, even though I cannot promise to make her happy."

David's lazy blue eyes narrowed, and he sat up stiffly.

"Do I understand that you intend to...?"

His voice died away in horror.

"Oh, quite. I thought you understood. May I introduce you? Inspector Blest, my future wife. Sit down, my young friend!" he added sharply as the young man lunged forward. "I do not want to have to shoot you. Bullet holes are such telltale affairs. But I shall do so unhesitatingly should it be necessary."

David subsided into his seat with the muzzle of the revolver only a few inches from his face.

"You—" he began.

"Hush, my dear sir." Saxon Marsh was mildly shocked. "I believe my fiancée is still unconscious, but, should she revive, I am sure you would not like her last memory of you to be connected with a string of profanities.

"I quite see your objection—the difference in our ages," he continued affably. "You young people are so often oversqueamish on that score. But I've had it in my mind for some time. Not unnaturally my friend Sir Leo, her guardian, did not see it in quite the same light as I did, but that, I am afraid, was because he did not altogether trust me."

"But you'll never get the money," David burst out angrily. "No English court would award it to you."

Saxon Marsh laughed aloud. "Fortunately it is not a case for an English court," he said. "That difficulty had arisen in both my own and Sir Leo's minds, when Major Deane was chosen for Miss Wellington, and Sir Leo very wisely transferred everything to France. No, my friend, I am afraid that you will go to your death knowing that I have beaten you in every way. When your body is washed up on some French or Spanish coast I shall be honeymooning in Paris. Really yours is a most distressing situation, Inspector."

David opened his mouth to reply, but the angry words never came, for the lookout man shouted a few words above the droning of the engine.

"Ah, the yacht," said Saxon Marsh, rising. "Not so fast, Inspector. I still have you covered."

Again David sank back, frustrated. The simple scheme which the sadist had detailed to him with such relish was so diabolically clever that he had no doubt but that it would succeed. He looked at Judy, and his heart failed him. He thought of the heartbroken Lionel Birch waiting in that fortress of a garden for the child who would never return. It was all the money, he thought bitterly, the wretched money. Had Judy only not been an heiress they might have been so inexpressibly happy. He dared not think of it. He longed desperately to take her in his arms, but always there was Saxon Marsh and the gun in the way.

From where he sat he could just see the yacht, a white speck in the searchlight's beam. As they drew a little closer he made out her beautiful slender form as she rode at anchor on the swelling tide. Her steam was up, he had no doubt, and he thought wretchedly of the scene which must inevitably follow.

They would be taken aboard. Perhaps he would be a corpse even before then. Judy would lie moaning in some overdecorated cabin, while his body would be pitched overboard at some convenient spot far away from the English shore.

It seemed to David that his whole life passed before him in

swift review, but in all those scenes it was Judy's face that looked up at him, Judy's face that smiled even through incidents which had happened long before he had ever met her.

And then, as the yacht loomed nearer and nearer and he was able to descry the details on her deck, another craft moved slowly out from behind her graceful white bows, a long low black craft lying close to the water, streamlined for excessive speed.

At the same moment that David caught a glimpse of it a tremendous white beam, much stronger than their own, cut through the grey night and bathed them in vivid light.

There was a shout from the man at the tiller, and David caught a glimpse of Saxon Marsh's distorted face as it was turned away from him for a second.

David's heart bounded. A police boat! Suddenly he realized the truth. Saxon Marsh had not got away quite so cleanly as he had supposed. It came to David in a flash of intuition that the efficient-looking police inspector of whom Marsh had spoken could have been none other than Inspector Winn. Somehow Winn had got on to Marsh and had then acted swiftly.

The police boat at the yacht was not waiting to rescue himself and Judy, but to capture an escaping malefactor.

As David recollected that low black craft, now completely hidden from their gaze by the dazzling beam of its own search-light, he realized that Marsh would have no hope of escape. Nothing could outrace that small black monster.

But he was not prepared for the tenacity and savagery of the man. Saxon Marsh rose slowly. There was an indescribable expression upon his cadaverous face. David caught a glimpse of his eyes and saw in them something he had only partly guessed. Saxon Marsh was a maniac, not to be taken alive.

The police boat was waiting, holding them in its vivid beam.

Saxon Marsh beckoned the lookout man, a huge, stupid-looking fellow who took the gun as he was told and held it trained on David. Saxon Marsh himself took the wheel.

The next moment the little boat was leaping through the water at full speed. The spray shot up on both sides, drenching all those within.

So he was going to make a run for it. David waited for him to swing the tiller round and wondered if the boat would capsize at the sudden swerve. But there was no turn, and with the recollection of that terrible expression in the small pale eyes still in his mind he suddenly realized the maniac's intention.

Saxon Marsh was speeding straight into the searchlight. He was going to murder them all.

The police boat seemed to guess his intention at the same moment. Without extinguishing its searchlight, it slid silently behind the yacht again. But Saxon Marsh hardly altered his course. He was bearing upon the yacht now, which waited for him, so graceful and yet not mobile enough to escape its owner's suicidal attack.

David shouted to the man in front of him.

"He's going to ram her!" he said. "Save yourself, man, for God's sake!"

The giant seaman wavered for an instant, and in that moment David sprang. His blow caught the man on the point of the jaw and sent him staggering back against the side, where he tripped and pitched backward into the water, an action which doubtless saved his life. The gun flew overboard and was lost.

They were almost upon the yacht now, and she seemed to tower up above them like a great white wall of death. The helmsman had already dived for safety, and David, bending forward, lifted the girl bodily in his arms, and, springing up upon the seat, leapt into the swirling water just in time.

A minute later there was a blinding, roaring crash. A sheet of flame seemed to leap out of the yacht's side, and all that was left of Saxon Marsh was flung back into the raging water, a burned and battered thing scarcely recognizable as a human form.

2 2

IN THE MORNING

S HE'S STILL ASLEEP, but she's all right. Thank God, my boy, she's all right."

The man who called himself Lionel Birch came down the rickety flight of wooden stairs and walked across the broad stone-flagged kitchen, his hand outstretched.

David took the proffered hand. It was nearly dawn. Outside the window the thin cold fingers of light were already beginning to creep over the cobbles and beached fishing boats of the little township to which the survivors had been brought.

Although it was so early in the morning, the scene in the big kitchen of the old-fashioned inn known as The Royal Fisherman was a picture of activity. The landlady, a tall East Coast woman in the sixties, had risen to the occasion.

The Royal Fisherman had seen thrilling rescues before in its four hundred years of life, and it kept up its tradition nobly. An enormous fire blazed on the hearth, food and hot drinks stood on a side table, and in the big chintz-hung, sweet-smelling bedrooms upstairs the local doctor and his assistants strove for the lives and health of those whom the sea had treated most roughly.

The yacht's crew had been taken off safely and were now

housed in the school farther down the village. Inspector Winn and his sea police colleagues were still out, searching for the mangled body of Saxon Marsh.

Ex-Sergeant Bloomer, another inspector, and two constables from the Hintlesham division who had come over by car in response to a telephone message from Winn earlier in the night were seated round the fire, warming themselves and waiting for his return.

David himself, looking pale and weary but still very much alive, if somewhat incongruous in a shirt and trousers belonging to the landlord, had been sitting with them.

Lionel Birch threw himself down into a chair and passed his hands over his eyes.

"It's over," he said. "She's safe. I can hardly believe it's true. I feel as if the last few years had been a series of terrible dreams, culminating in a ghastly nightmare from which I thought I should never awake. But when I looked at my girl just now lying there happy and peaceful and safe at last, I felt there was some good in the world after all."

There was silence after his voice had died away, and the three regular policemen nodded sagely. They were cheery, good-tempered fellows all of them, naturally a little excited by the thrilling events of the night and curious to hear the full story of the extraordinary crimes of which they had only heard the end.

Bloomer was frankly and unashamedly delighted with himself, and David, glancing at him, realized with a sudden flash of amusement that the old man was having the time of his life.

"It's a pity we didn't get the woman," he said. "It was mere chance we got the man. Of course, they may pick 'er up at the ports, but I doubt it. She's a slippery one. There's only one thing for it, Mr. Birch: you'll have to see Miss Wellington safely married before the year's out, and I don't suppose that'll be difficult."

He winked shamelessly at David, who, to his horror, felt

himself reddening awkwardly. Lionel Birch saw his change of colour and smiled.

"Still, you got the man, Sergeant Bloomer," he said. "That was very smart work."

Old Bloomer rose to the compliment like a fish to the bait.

"It wasn't bad," he said modestly, and hurried on as the Hintlesham police exchanged amused smiles. They realized that ex-Sergeant Bloomer's immediate circle was destined to hear the story of his deeds for ever and a day.

There was still no sign of Winn, and one of them generously gave him the lead.

"I can't think how you guessed he'd go back to the lonely house on the marsh, Mr. Bloomer," he said.

Bloomer sighed. He could tell the story all over again.

"Well," he said, taking his cigarette out of his mouth and blowing a luxurious cloud of smoke. "As soon as I saw the light I said to myself, 'If that's put there to guide the girl to 'er death, and it looks extremely like it, someone's got to put it out.' It's too dangerous to leave it there, I thought, for anyone seeing it after the young lady's drowned will think very much as I think and come to the same conclusions that I've come to."

"But not everyone's as clever as you, Mr. Bloomer," put in one of the Hintlesham constables, and received a black look from his inspector, who was a stickler for discipline.

Ex-Sergeant Bloomer did not notice the little comedy, however. He went on blissfully.

"Maybe not," he said. "But still, that's how I reasoned. So as soon as I'd rung up the Loo station and asked for a boat to be put out, I hopped on the motorbicycle belonging to Mr. Birch here and went down myself. Of course, I wasn't to know that the station boat wouldn't get there in time. I thought the young lady was as good as safe."

He paused and looked round.

"Well, as you know," he said, "I picked up a man, and we went to the lonely house where the light was still burning. As soon as I saw it I knew I was on the right tack. It was an enormous dry-battery torch, quite new, and one of the biggest I've ever seen. 'Someone'll come back for this,' I said to the Sergeant and of course 'e did, and we got 'im. And there 'e is in the Loo jail, where I hope 'e'll stay."

"Marguerite Ferney got away, did she?" said David thoughtfully.

Lionel Birch nodded. "The police interviewed the servants, but they could tell us very little. Apparently Webb was very clever. While the others were at the fair he motored off in the car which he and Miss Ferney had used all along and came back in twenty minutes. In the interval of the concert he remained talking to them. But after it was over he left Miss Ferney, meaning, no doubt, to pick her up when he returned with the lamp. He never came back. After a while she became anxious and set out on foot. She was never seen again. She must have found the little car abandoned on the moor and taken it. They may catch her, but somehow I doubt it."

The conversation was cut short by the entry of Inspector Winn. Looking at him, David felt all his old disapproval of the man vanish. Success became Inspector Winn much better than defeat. Success brought him generosity and good temper. It soothed his dignity and swept away all vestiges of the inferiority complex which had tended to make him a difficult working partner.

He came over to David and sat down.

"Found him," he said, "what was left of him. Not a pretty sight." He grimaced. "Still, a fitting end for a chap like that, and it saved the hangman a lot of trouble."

"The hangman?" David raised his eyebrows.

Winn slapped his knee. "Oh, of course, you don't know! Things have been moving, my boy. While you've been attending to this affair we've been busy on our end. I had a very good case out against Saxon Marsh for the murder of Johnny Deane, so we shan't have to go chasing our heads off after that elusive beggar Birch."

David and Judy's father exchanged glances. David rose to his feet.

"Inspector Winn," he said, "I should like you to have a word with me in the other room, if you don't mind. Will you come along too, sir?"

In the stuffy little inn parlour on the other side of the main doorway David effected a strange introduction.

"I only found it out myself this afternoon," he explained lamely, "and then the rescue of Miss Wellington seemed so imperative that I accepted her father's parole, and we went ahead."

Winn hesitated for a moment. Then he smiled. In the situation he could afford to be generous.

"Well, as it happened, it's all worked out very well, hasn't it?" he said. "There'll have to be a few official inquiries, Mr. Birch, you understand that, but I think I can safely say here and now that you've got nothing to fear."

Lionel Birch smiled.

"My dear sir," he said, "now that my daughter is safe I worry about nothing. Her worst enemy is dead, another is in jail, the woman who would have killed her is flying for her safety. There is only—" he paused, and added softly—"Thyn."

Winn glanced up. "Sir Leo Thyn," he said slowly, "was put under restraint at six o'clock this evening."

David swung round, his eyes alight with interest.

"Arrested? On what charge?"

Winn shook his head gravely. "He might have been arrested," he said, "and I imagine when his affairs are gone into, a warrant will be out for him if ever he's in a condition to have it served upon him."

"A condition?" Lionel Birch stared. "What do you mean?"

Winn shrugged his shoulders. "His nerve cracked. He went to

pieces. I thought he looked it when I saw him yesterday morning. Last time I approached the nursing home authorities before setting off for the yacht they told me what had happened. They didn't hold out much hope for recovery. But we shall see."

The silence which descended over the little room was broken by the arrival of the landlady. She put her head round the door.

"Miss Wellington is asking to speak to Inspector Blest," she said. "She seems quite all right, sir, but very anxious to see you."

"Go up, my boy. Go up at once." Lionel Birch touched David on the shoulder.

David went. He found Judy sitting up in a great chintz-hung bed. She was still very pale, and there were lines of strain round her eyes. But she was herself again. Hers was the true strength of health and youth which neither the machinations of Carlton Webb nor the ordeal through which she had passed could destroy.

She held out her hands. "David," she said.

He came over meekly and stood before her. "Yes, Judy?"

Now that he had come her courage seemed to have failed her.

"I wanted to thank you," she said, "for all you've done. You saved my life, David. I'm very grateful."

He hesitated awkwardly. The inclination to tell her that he loved her and to beg her to marry him was strong, but there was an obstacle in the way, and one which he felt he could never surmount.

"My dear," he said, forcing himself to speak lightly, "I could hardly have done any less, could I? You look awfully tired. Hadn't you better get some sleep?"

She looked at him with the eyes of a hurt child.

"What are you going to do?"

He laughed uncomfortably. "Well, as soon as Winn's rested we must go and make our report, and then I suppose I must get back to work. I've been on holiday, you know."

"Holiday!" said Judy, and they both laughed.

She held out her hand, and David forced himself to take it.

"I suppose this is good-bye?" she said.

"I—I suppose so," he echoed lamely, and added because he could not help himself, "I'll never forget you, Judy."

"Nor I you, David. Good-bye."

"Good-bye."

The word cost him an effort, and he moved hastily towards the door. On the threshold he paused. She had called him, and his name uttered softly and imploringly had only just reached him.

"David!"

"Yes?"

"Oh, David, is it—is it the money?"

He turned towards her, his face crimson.

"Yes," he said shortly.

"Need I take it?" Her voice was very small, and he came towards her and dropped upon his knees by the bedside.

"Oh, Judy, I love you. But you're an heiress, my dear, and a police inspector doesn't make a lot of money."

Judy put her arms round his neck.

"I've never had any of this wretched money," she said. "It's never brought me anything but wretchedness and danger, and I'm not going to let it take away the only thing I've ever really cared about in all my life. Besides, they tell me they haven't caught Marguerite Ferney. You'll have to marry me, David. You saved my life once. You may as well make sure of it. Finish the job, you know."

David looked at her helplessly.

"I don't know what to do," he said. "I love you so."

Judy sighed happily.

"That's all right, then," she said.

ABOUT THE AUTHOR

Margery Allingham, born in 1904 to Emily and Herbert Allingham, was an esteemed English novelist, author, and editor of *Christian Globe* and the *New London Journal*. Considered one of the four "Queens of Crime" from the golden age of detective fiction, Allingham began writing stories and plays at a young age and published her first novel, *Blackkerchief Dick*, at nineteen. She later studied drama and speech training at Regent Street Polytechnic in London. Allingham is best known for her character Albert Campion, a sleuth first introduced in *The Crime of Black Dudley*. Campion was featured in seventeen subsequent novels, and even more short stories. Allingham continued to write until her death on June 30, 1966.

MARGERY ALLINGHAM

FROM OPEN ROAD MEDIA

EARLY BIRD BOOKS

FRESH DEALS, DELIVERED DAILY

Love to read?
Love great sales?

Get fantastic deals on
bestselling ebooks delivered
to your inbox every day!

Sign up today at
earlybirdbooks.com/book

www.ingramcontent.com/pod-product-compliance
Lightning Source LLC
Chambersburg PA
CBHW020600030726
47497CB00007B/2025